THE SECRET WING

WING

FIFTH GRADE

TAL GOOD

CAFFEINATED TERRIER PRESS

This book is dedicated to all the black cats that sit on your keyboard and generally get in the way whenever you're trying to accomplish something.

Special thanks to the proofreaders who helped catch all the pesky typos that the faeries snuck into my writing, and I had absolutely nothing to do with:
Alfred Barten
Amy Christen
Anna Christen
Adrianne Gardner
Britt Goodman
Sophia Hartdegen
Sally Jenkins
Elly Vaughan
Carley Winn

CHAPTER 1

"Today's the day!" Liam said between panting breaths. He had barely been able to stop himself from crashing into Nora as he ran up.

"This isn't your bus stop. You're going to get in trouble," Nora said, but she was secretly glad to have her best friend with her for their first day of fifth grade. It was hard to believe the day was finally here after an extra-long summer break due to unexplained water damage in the hallway near the art room.

Pausing to catch his breath, Liam shook his head. "Nah, it's a new bus driver, not mean 'ol Skip. I'll just pretend I didn't know."

Liam turned to reveal his new backpack. Its bright, red canvas was drastically different from the faded blue one, which the two of them had "decorated" with scribbles and their names. It seemed like everything was changing, and Nora wasn't sure she was ready for it.

Following her eyes, Liam shrugged. "My dad threw the old one away. He said it was embarrassing. But, don't worry, I snuck it out of the trash to preserve our artwork. It's safely hidden under my bed."

"It's not a big deal." Nora said, but couldn't help but grin. She appreciated Liam's attachment to old belongings. Although, she didn't share his sentimentality. She was hoping to have a new outfit for the first day of school instead of her usual jeans and sweater. She hadn't even gotten new shoes this year, since both her moms insisted that she grow out of her old ones first. But looking down at the greying sneakers, she was hoping her feet would grow at least a little bit soon.

"Anyway, we're forgetting about what matters: The Secret Wing." Liam pulled a beaten-up journal from his backpack. Flipping through the lined-pages of sketches and notes, he stopped at one page. "Here it is!"

It was a crude drawing of a doorway off the side of their new school, one that did not connect to anything they had seen inside when they visited with their parents. Rumors had been circulating that the doorway led to a secret wing of the school, where specific students were taken to learn about supernatural subjects.

"We have to go through the door. Even if they don't bring us there. We've seen so many crazy things; we could at least share what we know." He began flipping through the notebook again. "There was that thing in the woods by your house, and the noise every night at the same time, and remember the stranger at the grocery store with an extra eye?!"

Knocking the notebook closed, Nora motioned to the school bus in the distance. "Liam, we promised we wouldn't tell people about these things.

Whenever we talk about them, things get stranger, and I just want to start at the new school without being the weird kids." As soon as she saw the hurt expression on Liam's face, she wished she could take the words back. Pinning back her shoulder-length brown hair with a barrette, she raised her eyebrows at Liam pleadingly.

"I never saw any of this stuff until you pointed them out..." Liam began, but the noise of the bus made the end of his sentence inaudible.

The school bus door opened to reveal their elderly bus driver, Skip. He grimaced at Liam and reprimanded him for being at the wrong pickup spot while promising Liam's parents would hear about it this time. Liam slumped his shoulders into his thick, blue hoodie and trudged to a seat as far away from Skip as he could. Nora followed and sat beside him.

"What is he doing here?! I thought we got a new bus driver," Liam groaned.

"Guess he just really likes us," Nora joked and a part of her was secretly glad that not everything had changed.

The girl in front of Nora, whom she recognized as being a year ahead of them, turned to see them both. "My mom said a lot of the bus drivers quit for some reason, so all the ones that were still here got shuffled around."

"Great, just my luck!" Liam said dramatically, "Skip will never quit. That guy just wants to make my life miserable."

The girl smiled sympathetically, and then turned back to her phone which she was playing a game on.

"Sixth-graders all have phones," Liam complained.

"Not all of them," Nora pointed to a boy in the front of the bus who was squinting through his thick glasses to see out the front window. Parts of his hair were sticking straight up, as if it were made out of pipe-cleaners, and although he was wearing shorts, his socks went up almost to his knees. Everything about his appearance from his clothing to the way he was sitting was bizarre.

"Right, AJ Splunker, Toilet Dunker, is just like every other sixth-grader. Get me some glasses so I can see my future better." Liam flopped back into the bus seat and shoved his knees into the seat in front of him causing the older girl to make a huffy noise.

"Just because AJ was picked on, a lot, by pretty much everyone when he was in our school, doesn't mean he still is. It's been a whole year, maybe things are different." While Nora made the suggestion, she watched AJ lean to the front of his seat and expose his batman underwear. "We'll probably have phones next year."

"I might have a chance if my parents get a divorce," Liam sighed, "wouldn't that be great? Otherwise they said I have to get straight A's, and we both know that will never happen."

Nora didn't respond. Her moms were always arguing about money, but she couldn't imagine them getting a divorce. She knew a phone was not in her near future, but she also wasn't as upset about it as Liam seemed to be. Sometimes when she saw the older kids, bent over, staring at their screens, she wondered if it was truly something she wanted for herself. It didn't look like as much fun as simply talking to a person. It was also the thing kids got in trouble for the most—having their phones in class.

"You're zoning out again," Liam said while poking Nora in the arm.

Nora frowned at Liam. "You know I hate it when you poke me."

As the bus rumbled on, Nora could feel the tension rising in her stomach. She began to scrutinize everything from the sweater and jeans she had chosen to wear to the way she had pulled her hair out of her face with childish, rainbow barrettes. Soon she would be surrounded by kids who were mostly older than her, since the new school went up to eighth grade. At least Liam would be with her and he seemed entirely unaware of the bus being filled with larger kids they did not recognize.

Once the new school came into view through the pine trees which surrounded it, Liam's mood improved drastically. He sat up and smiled at Nora, who reflexively smiled back. They streamed out of the bus, onto the front lot where students were waiting to be let into the expansive brick building. Some students were already in the grass, throwing pinecones at their compatriots. Most of them were much taller than both Liam and Nora.

"Finally!" Liam exclaimed, "Looks like some other fifth graders are gathering by the front steps, let's go somewhere else."

Nora agreed. There was no reason to draw more attention to themselves, so she followed Liam to the side of the building. They kicked pine needles through the grass while they walked to the side of the building. Vines of ivy crept up the bricks where trees had shaded it from direct sunlight. It was only when Liam continued past the side of the building that Nora began to panic.

"Liam, what are you doing?!"

"What do you think I'm doing? The Secret Wing." Liam continued walking with a purpose. He did not turn to see if Nora was following him.

"We can't go now. It's our first day of school!"

"That's exactly why now is the perfect time. If we don't find it, and we're late, we can just say we got confused and lost because it's our first day. Besides, Skip drives way faster than the other bus drivers, just about the only thing he's good for. We have fifteen minutes before they open the doors. I set my watch." Holding up his enormous digital wristwatch, Liam pointed at the minutes counting down.

Nora hoped that they would walk up to a locked door, find out it was a custodian's office and Liam would give up on the Secret Wing. But, there was a voice inside her that did not think it would be the case, and for some reason, she was excited about it. "Ok, fifteen minutes, but I really wish you would have warned me about this."

"You never would have come if I hadn't gone first. You're too cautious." Liam shrugged and led them around a jutting portion of the building.

They ducked under classroom windows, just in case a teacher happened to see them, and eventually came across the door they had seen through a window during orientation. It was much more peculiar up-close. The entire door was metal and painted black, but there were golden letters etched into the center. The letters read "Exter."

"What do you think that means?" Liam asked.

Without thinking, Nora brushed her fingertips over the letters, tracing the foreign word. As she did this, the door suddenly swung open. Liam and Nora jumped back, expecting an adult to appear and holler at them, but no one was there. The door pushed open to a regular-looking school hallway with tile floors and cement walls.

Liam shrugged and stepped up the few steps into the hallway without glancing back to see if Nora was following. Nora followed him and closed the door behind them, in case anyone passed by.

The hallway was nothing like what Nora was used to at her old school. There were no water-color art projects hanging on pink walls, just uninviting grey—a somber reminder she wasn't in grade school anymore. One of the fluorescent lights on the ceiling was flickering to its own rhythm, reminding her of a haunted house she had once regretted going into. Even Liam was hesitant to continue.

"We should go back," Nora whispered.

"No way, we got all the way here. We have to see what this is or we'll regret it forever." Liam took a few tentative steps forward.

Grabbing Liam's hand and pulling him down the hall, Nora said, "Fine. Let's get this over with, we only have eight minutes left." She was proud of her ability to see the countdown on his watch from a distance.

Liam allowed Nora to guide him down the hallway which seemed to be impossibly long until it branched out in two directions. To the left there was a low humming noise and to the right there was a short stairwell which led up to a glass-walled classroom. Thinking quickly, Nora pulled Liam to the left.

As soon as they walked into an entranceway, they discovered the source of the humming. A large fish tank took up most of the side of the room. Liam made a noise of excitement and moved closer to investigate. When Nora followed suit, she could see that the tank was full of luminescent jelly-fish. Floating like translucent hot air balloons, it was mesmerizing to watch them.

"Why would someone keep jellyfish in a school? Aren't they dangerous and hard to take care of?" Liam asked.

Squinting to see into the back of the tank, behind some of the fake plants and rocks, Nora swore she could see something lurking. A dark shadow passing between objects. "I don't think they're keeping the jellyfish as much as whatever's eating them."

"Eating them? Like a turtle?"

"A turtle?! Certainly not!" An unfamiliar voice of a woman from behind them caused Nora and Liam to leap almost a foot away from the tank.

The owner of the voice was wearing a black dress with white polka dots and her red hair was buzzed short on one side, while the other side went to her shoulder. Moving her hand to scootch up her thick-rimmed glasses, she examined them before saying, "You both better come with me."

Nora's chest filled with dread. They had been caught and were sure to be in for it. Her moms would be upset with her for causing trouble on her first day at a new school. For some reason, even though she was nervous about what was to come, her mind kept drifting back to the creature in the back of the tank. It was hard to get a good view of it, but it seemed to be made up of very dark, purple gelatin or perhaps it was covered in it. It had a discernable shape, even if it was not like one she had ever seen before.

The teacher brought her across the hall to the small, glass-encased classroom. Short bookshelves were in between three desks with laptops on them and there was a table with four chairs in the center of the room. To her surprise, two students were already sitting in the classroom, and one of them was AJ. He was at a table, holding a magazine too close to his face which made Nora wonder if his glasses were good for anything more than warping the size of his eyes. Next to AJ was a dark-skinned student with blue strands interwoven in his braids. He was intently taking apart some sort of electronic device with a screwdriver.

"You can call me Mrs. M." She pulled two packets out of a nearby bookshelf and dropped one on the table. "Here is your test," she said to Nora. "And you will come with me," she said to Liam while handing him the other packet.

Nora tried to say, "I don't understand..." but Mrs. M was already walking out the door guiding Liam to another room.

Was this some sort of a punishment or did she think they were different students? She never asked for their names. There was obviously a miscommunication. AJ and the other boy were actively ignoring her as they worked on their own activities. Looking down at the packet, it was some kind of sci-fi story. The title read, "The Terrible Case of the Orbs." That and the illustration of circles on the cover held Nora's interest. She flipped to the first page and read:

At dusk, we saw them.

People fleeing into the streets

Terrified and screaming

Searching for darkness—

For comfort.

She thought maybe it was one of those reading assignments where you read a poem and then answered questions, but there weren't any questions afterwards. It was just the strange words and what appeared to be a drawing of the shadows of people with white circles cut out of them.

"Searching for darkness—for comfort?" She muttered to herself. What did that mean? Was there something in the darkness that could comfort them? Or maybe it was the darkness itself?

When she examined the picture again, she suddenly realized they weren't artistic silhouettes. They were shadows. And the circles weren't cut out of them, they must have been orbs of light. Were the people covered in orbs of light? Then they truly were looking for darkness to comfort them.

'I think she's got it.' She heard the voice of AJ, but when she looked in his direction, his mouth hadn't opened.

CHAPTER 2

'Yeah, maybe, she wouldn't have come here otherwise.' It came from the other boy, but he wasn't speaking.

'There were two of them together, you know what that means.'

'It doesn't have to mean anything. Don't read too much into it.'

It was then that they noticed her gaping at them.

'I think she can hear us,' AJ said without opening his mouth.

"What's going on?" Nora asked.

"Wait, what am I thinking?" The boy with the braids said. 'What color should I do my hair next?'

"I like the blue, maybe red?" Nora answered.

AJ yelled, "Mrs. M!"

Mrs. M rounded the corner, her skirt expanding around her like a budding flower as she rushed in. "I know, I know. They got through the door, didn't they? Now both of you be on your way, I need to talk to Miss Nora Harte alone."

"Nora? I'm Cam, this is AJ. We're 6th graders," the boy said while following AJ to the door. "You'll meet the rest soon."

"Go on," Mrs. M said, closing the door behind them.

Nora was dumbfounded. She wanted to think about all of the possibilities of how it could all be a trick, but something in her knew it wasn't. She had heard their thoughts, and her mind was racing right along with her heart.

"I'm truly sorry, dear, it's a lot to take in," Mrs. M said while sliding a mug over to Nora. "I have made you some tea. We have a lot to discuss."

Nora took the tea and sipped it. It tasted like mint.

"I'm afraid I must be blunt. You are Wyrd."

Almost choking on the tea, Nora laughed. "Yeah, what else is new. I've always been weird."

"No, not weird, W-Y-R-D. It's what we call people who are special, different, entwined with fate—not that we believe in fate exactly, but more that you are destined to lead a spectacular and peculiar life due to innate abilities which manifest themselves at around your age." Mrs. M stopped to see if Nora was following her and then frowned. "Let me start over. Are you good at puzzles, changing perspectives, or seeing things that others overlook?"

Thinking back to Liam's notebook and all of the bizarre creatures they had seen this summer, Nora nodded.

"Good, well it's a gift that not all people have. You are one of only a half dozen in this school. We are very lucky to have found one-another. You will be taking separate classes here, throughout the day, in between your usual classes, to improve upon your gifts. Don't worry. We are informing your other teachers. Everyone will simply think you are taking extra courses to work on a subject you were struggling with."

"Special ed?" Nora dreaded the idea of people thinking she needed special education classes.

"Yes, and there is no reason for that expression. We do not have a stigma for them here. Students take them for all kinds of reasons. All of this aside, I have something very serious to talk to you about before I send you on your way." Mrs. M adjusted her glasses nervously and sighed. "Your friend."

"Liam?" Nora's heart skipped a beat. She had not even thought to ask where he was taken.

"I'm sorry to tell you this, but when a student, such as yourself, is Wyrd, it can cause a false awakening, of sorts, in those around them. In your case, your friend. He is not actually Wyrd like you, but because you have opened his eyes to everything, it is as if he is." There were deep lines in Mrs. M's brow when she frowned. Her dark eyes locked onto Nora's. "You have a difficult decision to make, Nora. If Liam discovers the truth, if you tell him that you are the one who is Wyrd and he is not, he will cease to be able to see things as we do. Bear in mind, it is not easy to be Wyrd. Many strange situations will occur, and you will have to come up with difficult solutions. It will likely alienate you from your classmates, and you will never be viewed as normal again. Would you wish this for your friend?"

There was too much to take in. Her mind was having trouble sorting through all of it. She was Wyrd, and something in her already knew it. She knew she would never be normal, but shouldn't Liam make the decision for himself. How could he make the decision, though? If what Mrs. M. was saying was true, if she told him, he wouldn't get to make any decisions. He had always been there with her, through everything since they were in first grade together. She couldn't even imagine learning about all of this Wyrd stuff without Liam.

"What if you talk to him about it?" Nora asked.

"I'm afraid that would only muddle things. You see, if he gets an inkling that one of you is not really Wyrd, then he may start asking you about it. The only way he will go back to a normal life, unable to see any peculiars, is if *you* tell him, since you are the one who opened his eyes to it. Whether you like it or not, the decision will eventually be yours to make, but we should not rush it." Mrs. M may or may not have been done speaking when there was a knock at the door. "We will continue this conversation at a later date, when you have settled in more and have had more time to think."

A heavyset man stood in the doorway, behind the glass, with Liam beside him. He rubbed a handkerchief over his red face and balding head and appeared to be mouthing words on the other side of the glass.

"Soundproof," Mrs. M smiled and waved at the man. "I truly am sorry to throw all of this at you so suddenly, but I feel this is something you need to know." She then opened the door.

"Hope you're all set. Don't want these two to miss their first class. Lucky for them, homeroom is extended on the first day." He then pulled two lollipops out of his pocket and handed one to Liam and one to Nora. "Little bit of candy couldn't hurt."

Liam took the candy, shrugged, and began eating his.

"Right, off you two go then. Mr. Walker will escort you to your classes. Don't talk about any of this where others can hear you. Go about your regular schedule. We will have class with the two of you tomorrow before lunch. Have a wonderful first day." Mrs. M waved goodbye and began tidying up the room.

Mr. Walker scurried ahead of them down the hallway. He had a unique way of shuffling his feet as he walked. They were going the opposite direction from where they had entered The Secret Wing, which did not surprise Nora. There had to be a way that the Secret Wing connected to the rest of the school.

'Liam, can you hear my thoughts, like the other kids?' Nora wondered.

'Yes! Wow, so much better than the two girls in the class I was in. They sounded all muffled or maybe they were just thinking too fast.' Liam grinned at Nora.

She could tell he was full of excitement. His notebook would soon be full of even more sketches of the Secret Wing. They turned several corners before exiting out of a door which was parallel to the art rooms, which Nora recognized by the old paint on several of the tables and art projects which had been discarded by their owners or put on display by the teacher.

'This is all so crazy. I can't believe it's real,' Nora thought.

'I know, aren't you glad I made you go there?'

Mr. Walker stopped abruptly. *'I want to make sure you two are aware that any other Wyrd within your vicinity will be able to hear you, before you manage to think up something embarrassing.'* One of his grey, bushy eyebrows rose as he eyed them. *'Also, any supernatural creatures that are nearby might be able to make out what you're saying and even be drawn to you. Please use caution.'*

Nora felt her cheeks burning and Liam gazed down at his sneakers as though he were being reprimanded.

Mr. Walker's voice was smooth and calm inside their heads. '*It is also easy to get distracted while your minds are chattering away. We are at Nora's homeroom. Try not to fret too much about all of this, you will understand more with time. We will be available should you need us. Do take care.*' He seemed sincere as he opened the door to Nora's homeroom and waved at the teacher.

The teacher, Nora recognized, was Mrs. Stokes, a math teacher whom she had met at orientation. Mrs. Stokes nodded at Mr. Walker and motioned Nora to the empty desk. The classroom was made up of students she recognized, whose last names were near hers alphabetically and sixth graders she vaguely remembered from years ago. The students were gathered into groups chatting. Chancing one last glance at Liam, she made her way to the empty desk on the side of the classroom.

"Nora, you've missed a lot of the new student orientation, where we discuss your schedule. We are now on freetime, so one of your classmates will have to bring you up to speed. Put all of this in your main notebook. Who would like to help Nora get her things in order with the last few minutes of homeroom?" The teacher scanned the classroom for a volunteer.

None of the students raised their hands. Nora began to feel sick.

"No one? Fine. I'll have to pick one of you."

"I'll do it," said a sixth grader with curly, blond hair. She sat with three other sixth graders and one fifth grader that Nora recognized. All of them were playing with some sort of dark purple slime to which they were adding sparkles.

The teacher smiled and nodded while Nora made her way over to their table. Opening the notebook, Nora began to examine the schedule and contents. She was not entirely lost, since they had gone through a mock schedule during orientation. However, they had never switched class-rooms in fourth grade, so it was a new experience and she was worried about finding the rooms.

The girls had been ignoring her and continuing to play with their slime.

It almost startled Nora when the girl with curly hair spoke. "You came in with the Sped teacher, so that makes you *special,* huh? Have trouble finding homeroom?" Her face contorted into an ugly sneer when she spoke. "Aw and she's even got rainbow barrettes, like we used to wear in kindergarten."

The other girls laughed menacingly. Without meaning to, Nora's hand went to her barrette and she could feel her face grow warm. She desperately wanted to run away from them. While they gawked at her tauntingly, she gave up the idea of asking them any questions about her schedule or the school.

"What, you can't talk either?" Another girl jeered. "You're right, Jess. Maybe we need to talk *s-l-o-w-e-r* so she understands us." She said, stretch-ing out the last words in the sentence.

The other girls snickered. Meanwhile, Nora tried to make eye contact with the fifth-grader who used to sit near her in grade school. Her name was, "Penelope," and she had always been shy but nice. Penelope was doing her best not to turn her attention away from the slime.

"Thanks so much for your help," Nora finally said loudly and got up, but as she did, her backpack snagged her chair and knocked it loudly to the floor.

The entire classroom got quiet except for the girls who were now guf-fawing. Before Mrs. Stokes could intervene, the bell rang and students began rushing to their first class. Sighing, Nora lifted the chair and made her way to English class. She just had to sit through one class and then she would be in Science with Liam where they could talk about everything that had happened, including the girls who were mean to her.

Slipping her barrettes out of her hair, she tossed them into her backpack with the rest of her belongings. '*No stigma for special ed, huh?*' she thought grumpily on her way to her class and could have sworn she saw an older girl turn to look at her.

Chapter 3

The science room had big, black tables that were impossible to damage, and the science teacher let them sit wherever they wanted for the first day. Nora was relieved to find Liam already waiting for her and pointing at the chair next to him.

"The girls in my homeroom were really mean," she blurted out when she joined him.

"Really?" Liam responded as if he wasn't expecting a conversation.

"Yeah, they made fun of me for coming in with Mr. Walker."

"Sounds like they're just jealous," Liam scoffed. He slid his notebook out of his bag. "I started sketching already, but we should compare notes after school. I could just get off the bus at your house..."

'*Not with Skip as our driver,*' Nora thought.

'Ah! This is so cool! We will never get in trouble for talking during class, and we can say whatever we want, like the fact that the science teacher has a hole in the back of his pants.' As Liam thought this, the science teacher turned around abruptly and loudly started the day's introductions. Liam's eyes grew wide, wondering if he had been overheard.

'I think that was a coincidence. Nora thought. But we really shouldn't test it. We have no idea which students or teachers are Wyrd. Also, I can't focus on anything our teacher just said while we're doing this.'

'Yeah, you're right. I didn't even catch his name.'

'It's written on the board.'

"Liam? Liam Kelly?" the teacher was repeating his name.

Nora nudged him.

"Huh? Oh, yeah." Liam replied.

"Please just say 'here,' like the other students." The science teacher sighed as the class began to snicker.

"Right, sorry." Liam said.

The rest of the day went on without a hitch. Nora found all of her classes. The other fifth-graders were just as nervous and confused as she was or worse. Most of her teachers seemed friendly, especially the art teacher who was eccentric and energetic. She was actually excited about her classes, and she had lunch with Liam. Although they both wanted to talk about the Secret Wing during lunch, it was not hard to focus on all of their new experiences in their classes. Lunch always seemed too short and there was a large area in the back of the school to explore during recess with wooden walkways and playground equipment. Once they understood the layout of the backyard a little better, Nora was certain they would be able to find a spot to talk about the Secret Wing— away from eavesdroppers, but for now, she and Liam agreed to wait until they were home.

At one point, Nora passed Cam, the boy she met in the secret wing, and she thought she saw him wink at her, but it was hard to tell. Her last class of the day was history and after all of the excitement from earlier and the warmth of the sun coming in through the high windows in that room, Nora found herself nodding off and missing most of the class before she even realized it.

When they boarded the school bus to head home, Skip's grimace was especially pronounced through all of his wrinkles. It was as if to say, "you better not cause trouble."

Liam and Nora moved to the back, and she saw AJ sit in the front seat. He did not acknowledge them and was scooched up to the front edge of his seat, just as before, so he could lean forward and stare out of the windshield.

Liam anxiously chatted about his classes and teachers, but Nora knew he was burning to talk about the Secret Wing. He fidgeted beside her like a bag of popcorn in the microwave. She was also having trouble containing herself. As soon as the bus reached Liam's stop, he jumped up and ran to the front to be scolded by Skip for running.

Each stop before Nora's seemed to be excruciatingly slow. She sat on the edge, like AJ, ready to get up as soon as her stop came up. As she rushed to the door, she heard a familiar voice in her head.

'*Be careful*,' was all AJ said.

She did not look at him, but nodded to acknowledge what he had thought to her and got off at her stop. Then she wondered what he was referring to. Was it just to keep the Secret Wing a secret or was there something else he was trying to warn her about? It seemed strange that he would wait until the end of the bus ride to say something. Before she could put any more thought into it, she noticed Liam in the distance. His cheeks were red as he puffed his way down the road to her bus stop. It was hard not to smile while she waited.

Once Liam reached her, he nearly collapsed trying to catch his breath. "I...can't...believe...what...happened!"

'*You don't have to talk, remember?*'

'*Oh, yeah, this is so much easier.*'

After Liam caught his breath, they made their way down the road to Nora's house. The dark brown dwelling almost blended into the trees which surrounded it on the dead end road. It was the only home Nora ever knew, and although her moms had assured her younger sister and her that they would not be moving, Nora felt as though the future were uncertain.

When they opened the door, Nora moved it slowly so as not to creak too loudly. She put her hand to her lips to instruct Liam to be quiet. '*Momma G's working tonight, so she's still asleep.*' Not having to talk really was convenient.

They made their way downstairs, where they could speak freely. Liam immediately pulled out his notebook to reveal sketches of the door and the hallways they had walked through in the Secret Wing. He had also started sketching the fishtank they saw. They both sat on the beige carpet of the basement floor and examined the drawings.

"What happened to you when we separated?" Nora had been curious about it all day.

Liam's blue eyes shifted to the ceiling as he tried to recall all of the details. "Mrs. M brought me to a classroom. It wasn't glass like the one you were in, and it was on the other side, past the fishtank. There were two girls there; they were older, seventh and eighth grade. Then she put this weird story in front of me. I think it was about goblins. I mean, there was all this crazy stuff going on, but in the picture, it made me think of some gobliny creature. Like maybe they lived there first and people did things that woke them up or disturbed their environment. I don't know, but I was really focused on the story and there were these muffled noises, like people talking loudly on the other side of the wall. So, I started looking around to figure out where the talking was coming from and I realized it was the girls. I couldn't hear their thoughts very clearly, but it had to do with something that had happened last year at the school."

Liam turned his attention to Nora when he finished, and she realized she had been staring at him while trying to discern every detail.

He continued, "I kind of got the impression that something crazy happened and they were scared to talk about it."

Nora couldn't keep it to herself any longer.

"Hey, Liam?" She asked.

"Yeah?"

"Are you sure you want to keep doing this stuff? I mean, it could be dangerous, and it could screw up our classes. Those girls were making fun of me for being with the special ed teacher and we got you in trouble during science class already. I'm just saying, if you had the option, would you want to just forget about all the Secret Wing stuff? Meeting Liam's eyes, she made sure he understood what she was saying.

"What? Are you kidding? Of course, I'm going to keep going to the Secret Wing. This is the most exciting thing that has ever happened to me. And we might finally get some answers for all the strange stuff that's happening. But, I guess I'd understand if you didn't want to. I mean, I'd still be friends with you. I get that this stuff is kind of scary." Liam returned Nora's gaze.

At this point, Nora wondered if Liam had been given the same speech she had been given by Mrs. M. Perhaps he was the one who was Wyrd and had caused her to see all of this. Or maybe Mrs. M simply didn't know which one of them was Wyrd and it was her way of getting them to work it out. Either way, if this was what Liam wanted, Nora would not abandon him. They had stuck together this far, and there was no way she would let him go it alone.

"No, I want to do this too. I just think we need to stick together, because I have a feeling things are going to get harder." Nora often heard herself warning or saying foreboding words to Liam, but this time it seemed like he actually took them in.

"Best friends forever," Liam nodded, bumping fists with Nora, as was their usual response.

Suddenly, they were interrupted by a noise so loud that it had to be either a bowling ball dropped down the stairs or someone who had no regard for how loud their footsteps were. Nora's younger sister came racing down and flopped onto the couch behind them.

"Emaline! You're being too loud! You're going to wake up mom!"

Emaline kicked off her shoes and put her bare feet on Nora's back while sticking her tongue out and blowing raspberries.

"You are so lucky you don't have a younger sister," Nora said while knocking her sister's feet off of her.

"I wouldn't mind having at least one brother or sister, though. It kind of sucks being an only child." Liam shrugged and put his notebook into his backpack while pulling out a well-worn, blue baseball hat and covering his messy, blond hair with it.

'*Yeah right,*' Nora thought, '*being an only child is great. You get everything to yourself.*'

'*Your sister's not so bad. It can get pretty lonely at my house. Why do you think I'm always here?*'

"Why are you two staring at the wall? Did middle school make you stupid?" Emaline asked in a squeaky voice, the one she used just to irk her big sister..

'*Not so bad, huh?*' Nora thought with a quick glance at Liam, and then said, "Yep, we're stupid now. Guess you should stop talking to us."

'*This is good practice. We need to get better at thinking to each other without looking like we're daydreaming or doing something else.*' Liam thought.

"I know how to fix it." Suddenly Emaline wacked Liam in the back of the head with a pillow, sending his hat flying.

"That's it, you have declared war!" Liam yelled.

Liam grabbed Emaline, restraining her so Nora could tickle her. They tortured Emaline until she screamed that she would pee her pants, but as soon as they let go of her, she was back to hitting them with pillows and causing general chaos. Both of them tried their best to send thoughts to one another, but they were scattered causing them to react too slowly to catch a pillow or even an elbow. Before long, Nora's fears became reality, and Momma G woke up. A scruffy voice hollered at them from up the stairs and they were immediately silent.

"Take it outside!"

"Great," Nora threw her hands up in the air. "I told you to be quiet. You woke up mom."

"Me?! It's not my fault. You two were being weird!" Emaline folded her arms across her chest, pouting.

"NOW!" Momma G roared.

CHAPTER 4

The three of them scrambled over each other to get their shoes and jackets on while heading out the door into the backyard. They walked by the rusty playset and straight into the woods behind their house. There was always something to do in those woods, no matter how small they were. They could use sticks to free up blockages in the stream that ran through it, go scrounging for cool rocks, or hang out in the leftover foundation from the old abandoned shed out back.

"I told you, you were being too loud," Nora said glaring at her sister who was stomping over dried twigs.

"I don't care!" Emaline yelled and stuck her tongue out. "You two were being weird."

'*She's onto us,*' Liam thought.

"I wish you wouldn't be such a brat," Nora said.

"I wish you wouldn't be such a know-it-all!" As Emaline said this she picked up a stick and threw it at Nora.

It hit Nora's leg. "Quit it!"

"Make me!" Emaline said while throwing another stick.

Liam put his hands together pleadingly "OK, OK, why don't we just calm down and..."

"Shut up!" Emaline and Nora said in unison.

Liam shrugged and they continued walking toward a fort they had been working on during the summer. There were a few old boards they had found in the woods, but it was mostly large sticks tied together. Some leaves had fallen off of the trees early and crunched noisily beneath their feet as they walked, but none of them spoke as they headed toward their destination. It was then that Nora thought she heard something — a bizarre, almost mechanical noise.

"Wait, stop for a second. Did you two hear that?" She held up her hand to indicate for them to stop walking.

The three of them waited for a few seconds, shrugged and were just about to continue when the noise came back, this time louder. It was eerie, almost like the sound of a broken machine grinding two pieces of metal together. Emaline's eyes were so wide that Nora could see the white all around them. She instantly had an urge to stand by her sister, protectively. Liam turned his head trying to identify the sound.

"We have to go see what it is," he said.

"I don't know if that's such a good idea," Nora began to say, but found herself already following after Liam. Emaline was now clutching onto Nora's arm tightly as they walked.

There was another noise. This time it was muffled and high pitched, like a baby crying from far away. They stopped to listen, as soon as the noise stopped, they continued in its direction. Nora scanned the area ahead of them. There was the broken-down structure in the distance that they assumed was a shed at some point. Some of the boards for their fort had been purloined from it, but it was mostly a crumbling foundation with a few stray pipes. When Nora had asked her moms what it was, they shrugged and said it hadn't been used for a very long time.

As they grew closer to the old foundation, the bizarre noise started up again and grew louder. Liam took hesitant steps around the side of the structure, trying to walk as quietly as possible on twigs and dead leaves. Nora kept her distance behind him with her sister beside her.

"Oh," Liam finally said as he got around the corner.

"What is it?" Nora asked, moving up closer to get a better vantage point.

There was a raccoon, puffing up its fur and growling while chomping on a rusty drainpipe. As soon as it saw them, it reeled backwards and rushed up a nearby tree. Emaline laughed and released Nora's arm from her grasp. Relief washed over them and Nora smiled at how adorable the fluffy raccoon was, up the tree out of their reach.

"What was it doing?" Nora asked.

Liam knelt down to examine the pipe. It was then that they heard the high-pitched whine again. Joining Liam at the pipe, Nora bent down and peeked inside. She could barely make out the reflection of tiny eyes staring back at her.

"There's a baby raccoon in there," Nora exclaimed, "I think it's stuck!"

Emaline gasped. "We have to get it out! What are these stupid pipes doing out here anyway?"

Nora nodded in agreement.

"I can probably reach it," Liam offered.

"You can't just touch it with your hands, Liam, you'll get rabies or something." Upon seeing skepticism on Liam's face, she made sure to add, " and even if you don't get rabies, you'll have to get a whole bunch of rabies shots. That happened to this kid Ben, in my class. He tried to pet a opossum and it bit him and when he pulled away it dragged all the way down and cut up his arm and he had to get a shot for every inch." Emaline babbled on and on before putting her hands on her hips and nodding matter-of-factly like she had won an argument.

"I don't think opossums carry rabies all that often," Nora said.

"I'm not lying!" Emaline insisted, stamping her feet.

Liam obviously couldn't take much more of the bickering. "Fine, fine! No one said you were. What do you suggest?"

"Gloves?" Nora asked.

"Oh! I put Momma T's gardening gloves in the fort. I'll be right back!" Emaline rushed away before Nora could respond.

The raccoon remained in the tree, watching them intently. It was obviously stressed about its baby, but would not chance going near them. Nora wished there was something she could do to reassure the raccoon, but she knew it wouldn't understand.

"If we had a phone, we could take pictures of this," Liam offered.

"I'm sure you'll end up drawing all of it, and I like your drawings better anyway."

Liam smiled at Nora and pulled his notebook out. "I should get started on it then." He began to sketch out the pipe and the structure. He drew a fuzzy outline of the raccoon, intending to fill in the details later.

Emaline returned noisily and handed the thick gloves to Liam. They bent down and Liam got onto his stomach. He peered into the tube once, before shoving his gloved hand down it and snaking his arm in afterwards.

By the time he was in the pipe all the way up to his shoulder he said, "I think I have it," and added, "there's a lot of mud in here."

'*Ok, slide out slowly,*' Nora thought, '*and try not to think about the bugs.*'

'*Bugs?! Why didn't you warn me about bugs? Yuck!*' Liam began to pull back slowly until he was out to his elbow and then stopped.

'*What are you doing?*'

"I think I'm stuck," he said, tugging.

Nora grabbed Liam around the waist and pulled as hard as she could. He didn't budge.

"Oh no," Emaline exclaimed.

Just then, the raccoon bolted down the tree in their direction. Nora let out a startled yelp and pulled on Liam just as he was leaping back to get away from the mama raccoon who was rushing at them, growling with her teeth barred. In the sudden jolt of chaos, Liam's elbow popped free of the pipe and he fell backwards on top of Nora. They were stunned for a minute; both had the wind knocked out of them.

A little, muddy ball sat on Liam's hand. It was too exhausted or scared to move, but stared at them with its dark eyes.

'*Would you get off of me?*' Nora thought before she could talk.

'*Sorry,*' Liam thought back.

"It's soooo cute!" Emaline squealed.

The mother raccoon stood a foot away from them, growling, hissing, and making all kinds of noises they had never heard an animal make.

'*It's OK, we're trying to help,*' Nora thought.

All of a sudden, the raccoon was no longer growling. It sat down and watched them intently.

"Why did she just calm down like that?" Emaline asked, stepping out from behind the tree she had been hiding in back of.

Liam exchanged glances with Nora. "You think she'll let us wash him off a little in the stream?"

"Maybe? Are we sure there aren't any others?" Nora wondered. She inspected the pipe, but didn't see any more reflective eyes. "Ema can you go get a flashlight so we can be sure?"

"No way, I wanna help wash the cute little baby!" Emaline yelled.

"Although, don't raccoons wash their food before they eat it?" Liam pondered, "She may think that we're getting ready to eat it."

"How on earth do you know that?" Nora did not want to offend Liam, but he wasn't exactly a big reader or the kind of kid that paid attention in Science class.

Liam explained. "There's this really funny video with a raccoon and cotton candy where he tries to wash it and it disappears. Well, now that I'm thinking about it, it's kind of sad actually."

Nora sighed. '*We're going to get him clean,*' she thought to the raccoon, and somehow it seemed to understand. The stream was very close to where they were, and the raccoon mother followed them, staying a few feet away at all times. Nora wasn't sure if the raccoon comprehended what she had thought or what they were doing, but somehow she was able to convey that they were not going to hurt the baby.

Liam dipped the baby raccoon into the water and used his gloves to remove chunks of mud until it began to appear less like a mud ball with eyes and more like a drenched rat. As soon as it was able to move its arms and legs, Liam knelt down and placed it gently on the ground. In the most adorable way possible, it grabbed at its ears with its tiny hands to clean more dirt off. Once the three of them backed away, the mother scooped the baby up and rushed to a nearby tree without taking her eyes off of them.

"Goodbye cute raccoons, I wish I could have petted you, but I don't want to get a million rabies shots like Ben," Emaline said as they left.

Afterwards they got flashlights and tools and spent an hour digging mud out of the pipe, and breaking off pieces of it with shovels to make sure there weren't any more raccoons inside. They didn't find any more fuzzy animals, but they did find a vast array of insects and spiders that caused Liam to shudder and double check his arm repeatedly. Once they were all thoroughly covered in mud, they agreed it was likely almost time for dinner.

They congratulated one another on a job well done by patting clumps of dirt off of their backs while saying their goodbyes, fully knowing that as soon as they returned home, their parents would be less than thrilled about the mess.

CHAPTER 5

The next morning, Nora found Liam anxiously awaiting her on the school bus. He had tried to sit as far back as he could, but there were other students who got on before him so the pickings were slim. Nora sat next to Liam and noted the disheveled hair sticking out of his baseball cap and the tag in the front of his shirt. Lack of sleep was obvious from the dark bags under his eyes to the constant yawning.

"What happened to you?" Nora asked.

"Hmm? Oh, I spent most of the night drawing the raccoons and writing about everything that happened yesterday. Wasn't it crazy? I wonder if we can talk to animals now?" Liam chattered on without paying any mind to who may be listening.

'I don't think so,' Nora thought, *'And we don't want anyone overhearing this.'*

'*What about him?*' Liam thought back as AJ got onto the school bus.

Nora shrugged, but thought she saw AJ turn his head slightly in their direction. '*I don't think animals understand us really, not the words exactly. It was more like the emotions. She got that we weren't going to hurt her.*'

'*Ok, not as cool, but could be useful. We'll have to experiment with it more, too bad neither of us have any pets.*' Liam pulled out his notebook, which seemed to be filling up fast and jotted down a few more notes before yawning again. '*Oh, sorry, I didn't mean to bring up Molly. It's nice not sneezing at your house though.*'

Nora's cat, Molly, had passed away last year. Molly was older than she was, but it was still hard on her whole family. She missed her cat and didn't want to think too much about it.

'*You really are a mess. Your shirt's inside-out and backwards.*' Nora pointed out.

'*What?*' Liam looked down and immediately began to pull off his shirt and straighten it.

Suddenly the bus jerked to a halt. After pulling the bus over to the side of the road, Skip stood up and pointed his finger toward the back. To Nora's shock, Skip was pointing directly at her and Liam. "What do you think you're doing?! You can't just undress on my school bus! You two are too young for those kinds of shenanigans!"

Liam's face was as red as a fresh apple, and Nora felt her own face burning too. She couldn't be more mortified at what Skip was inferring. She wanted to leap into another seat, but couldn't move.

"That's not..! My shirt was on backwards!" Liam yelled.

"Likely story, I'm telling the principal. You two will be staying after. And just for that, we're going to have assigned seating from now on!" Skip said, his scowl wrinkling his entire face to the point where his beady eyes were barely visible.

The other students on the bus groaned.

"You can all blame the love birds over there. Move to another seat, now, young lady!" Skip didn't wait to see Nora comply. As he turned, his wispy, white hair flew around him like dandelion puffs.

Nora rushed to an empty seat and sunk down as far as she could. Hiding her face, she did not want anyone to see the embarrassed tears welling up.

Liam opened his mouth to say something else, but then they could both hear AJ.

'Don't. Don't say anything. It'll just make things worse.' AJ thought to them.

Liam shut his mouth and slumped down just like Nora did. Neither of them would chance a glance at one another. The bus rumbled on to the school and slowly the chatter of the other students returned.

'What a jerk,' was the only message Liam was able to convey to Nora. Nora was unable to respond. She was too upset and just wanted to hide somewhere.

As soon as the bus screeched to a halt, Nora rushed to the front and down the steps. She refused to make eye contact with anyone and headed straight to the side door of the Secret Wing without checking to see if anyone was following her. When she reached for the door, she could hear Liam.

"Nora, wait, you can't just go straight there. What if someone saw us going around the side of the building? And what about homeroom?" He hesitated when he saw the tears on her cheeks.

"I don't care!" Nora blurted out. "I can't go to homeroom! Those mean girls will hear about this by then and it'll be awful!"

"Nora, I'm sorry, I didn't know that would happen."

"I think we should just stay away from each other for a while, I mean, until the rumors go away." She was still avoiding looking at Liam, but she could tell by his voice that he was hurt.

"What? No! I'm not going to stop hanging out with you just because of some stupid bus driver. We're best friends. Why do you care so much about what people think?"

"I don't," Nora said automatically.

"Then why aren't you wearing your barrettes anymore? You got them at Pride with your moms, and they're your favorite." Liam pointed at Nora's brown hair, she had tucked behind her ears.

If he had wanted to make her feel worse, he had succeeded. She knew he wasn't implying that she didn't want people to know she had two moms, but it still stung. She was proud of her family and always would be. It was just that they were in a new school full of older kids. Why couldn't Liam try to fit in once in a while?

"I don't want people talking about us. It's just so...*embarrassing*."

"What's so embarrassing about it?"

Before Nora could answer, AJ stepped over to them. "It's OK," he said, "I'm sure Mrs. M will cover for you if you don't want to go to homeroom. But, you probably shouldn't both ditch. It would look weird."

Liam glared at AJ and threw up his hands. "Fine! I don't care!" He then balled his hands and thrust them into the pocket of his hoodie so hard that Nora could see his knuckles pointing through them before stomping back to the front of the building where the other students were waiting for the doors to open.

AJ handed Nora a tissue. But when she went to accept it, his hand shocked hers. She thanked him all the same.

"Sorry, that happens to me a lot," he said referring to the shock, "I always have tissues, because I'm allergic to dust and grass pollen and tree pollen and mold and chemicals. Also nuts and dairy and gluten." As he listed all of his allergies, he led Nora into the Secret Wing.

The hallway was longer than Nora remembered it, and AJ was just as nerdy as she had always assumed. His checklist of allergies continued endlessly with him going into too much detail about what each allergen did to his body. The only tolerable thing about his rambling was that it managed to take her mind off of the bus incident.

By the time Nora's patience had completely worn thin of AJ, they discovered Cam in the glass room talking to Mrs. M, who was wearing a green dress with watermelon slices printed on it. A lime green belt was tied tightly around her thin waist, causing the skirt to flare out. And Nora could have sworn the longer side of her hair had switched from the right to left side.

"I believe I was clear about students going to their homeroom before coming here," Mrs. M said plainly.

"She was having some trouble with Liam," AJ started.

"I don't see how that matters."

"On the *bus*," AJ emphasized the last word and nodded to Mrs. M knowingly.

Mrs. M's expression softened, and she gave AJ an affirming glance. "Ok, then, Nora, I will let your homeroom teacher know we needed to go over paperwork. In the meantime, you can help Cameron with his current project. AJ, come with me." Mrs. M's high heels clicked noisily as she walked out of the room, f with AJ following in the wake of her swirly dress.

Cameron's hair was now interwoven with red extensions. He smiled at Nora and motioned for her to sit across from him at the table in the center of the room. When she was seated, Cameron tilted the paper he was examining so it was sideways to both of them. It was a detailed map of the school with architectural notes. Cameron had circled several areas with chalk.

"So, um, I've been noticing stuff going missing for a while. Weird stuff, like not just pencils and things that people would want. Wrappers, used gym socks, half-eaten sandwiches." He pulled his sleeves down over his hands and zipped up the puffy blue vest he was wearing. "Is it cold in here?"

"Not really," Nora shrugged. "Did this just start? Could it be a new cleaning-person?"

"Nah. This is from last year. Although yesterday was the worst of it. Tons of kids were complaining about missing things. I was thinking maybe it was a Lutin, but there wasn't any hair stuff going on." Pulling a large encyclopedia off of the shelf, Cam dropped it on the table with a thunk and turned to a bookmarked page. There was a picture of a knobby, green goblin pulling a girl's hair.

Nora turned to the front of the tome and saw it was the "Encyclopedia of Mythological Creatures." It was larger than any encyclopedia she had ever seen. The hard cover was worn around the edges, but the gold text still glittered. Generally every school had a few encyclopedias kicking around, but no one used them unless they couldn't get on a computer to look up information. "I've never heard of any of these things," she said, while flipping through the pages.

"No one has, really. That's what the book's for. I'm trying to narrow down where the thing's taking all the stuff it steals, but I also need to find out what it is to know how to deal with it…I could really use some help." He pointed at the map, "I've narrowed down the main areas of the school where people don't go: storage rooms, closets, stuff like that. There's more than you would think."

"That *is* a lot. How are you narrowing them down?"

"I just started, but I was planning to snoop around these areas, follow any trails. Not really sure, honestly." Sitting in the chair across from Nora, he watched her expectantly, as if she would know how to continue.

"Most of them are probably locked, and until we know what it is, we probably don't want to charge right in. Some of these, like the storage under the bleachers, might be dusty, and a creature would probably leave footprints, so we could look for that. We could also follow patterns of where and when things are going missing." Nora realized she was thinking out-loud and suddenly felt a little self-conscious that she was talking to Cam the way she would Liam.

"Wow, you really are one of us. You're made for this. Let's check out the bleachers today before 5th-grade recess. It's when your lunch gets out and mine starts, so no one should miss us if we're late." Cam was grinning down at the map as if he had achieved something.

Although he seemed to have missed the part when Nora said it wouldn't be a good idea to charge right in, she had a feeling pointing that out would be about as good as all the times she tried to keep Liam from rushing into situations. So, her best bet was to find out what sort of beast it was. How many possible monsters would hide in a school and steal garbage? Flipping through the encyclopedia, she saw all kinds of creatures with detailed, color drawings of their multiple clawed limbs, leathery wings or glowing eyes. Some were more frightening than others. Narrowing down the search would be a lot harder than she thought.

She had to show this book to Liam; he would love it. Probably spend hours leafing through the intricate drawings. But, then she remembered what she had said to him this morning. He might be angry with her for suggesting they avoid one another for a while. She realized it was likely a good idea to avoid being seen with any of the students from the Secret Wing, so as not to draw suspicion from the other students, even though there were so few of them and they were all in different grades.

"See anything useful?" Cam asked, noticing Nora had been on the same page for a while.

"No, I was just thinking about how there's barely any Wyrd students. There's only one in seventh and one in eighth. How many were there last year?"

Cam shifted in his seat and his hair fell over his face. "Uh, something happened. We don't talk about it. Looks like the first period is starting. I'll see you after your lunch. Don't forget." Scooping up his backpack and whatever he had left on the table, Cam rushed out of the glass classroom.

Watching him leave with a bit of confusion, Nora remained in her seat as Liam and another girl entered with Mrs. M. She was older, but not much taller than Liam and was wearing a shirt with an anime character on the front.

"Nora, I wanted to introduce you to Kimi. She's going to be your seventh-grade buddy," Mrs. M explained. "As you may recall from orientation, the fifth-graders get a seventh-grade buddy to show them around and spend time with them occasionally, and the sixth-graders get an eighth-grader. We try to match up our own students when we can to give them an excuse to be seen together."

"Hey." As Kimi waved, her multiple bracelets clinked together.

Liam sat in a seat on the far end of the table, and Nora instantly felt her chest tighten. While Kimi took a seat next to Nora, Mrs. M stood in front of a whiteboard.

"Welcome to your first day of Wyrd Class. We have a lot to go over, so I won't delay. Questions are welcome when you think of them, so please raise your hand. Now, this classroom is sound-proof, as you know, so we will be conducting many of our classes here. All of the books throughout the room hold forgotten lore. Although we are not worried about outside students or teachers taking them seriously, they are quite old and we do not want them misplaced, so they are to remain in the classroom or library."

Mrs. M spoke quickly without pausing to make sure the students were keeping up with her. "We will have scheduled class periods, but I am aware it may be of the utmost importance for you to come here when not scheduled. Just try not to do it too often, and we can come up with excuses for your other teachers. I am aware that this is a lot to take in, so I have invited Mr. Walker to speak with you for a few minutes before we continue." When Mrs. M finished speaking she took a seat beside the whiteboard and watched the door expectantly.

After an awkward silence with no one wanting to make eye-contact with anyone else, Mr. Walker came rushing into the classroom. He was breathing hard and his face was flushed. He pulled a handkerchief out of his pocket and wiped his forehead before standing in front of the whiteboard. "I am so sorry I'm late, Mrs. M. I am very happy to be able to talk with Liam and Nora and it is nice to see you, Kimiko. As you all know, I work in the

East Wing here, but I am also one of the school counselors. We all know how stressful middle school can be all by itself, especially when coming to a new school, but it can be even more difficult for Wyrd students. I want you to know that you can talk to me about any of your problems. It's a judgment-free zone. I have resources to help you with academic problems, interpersonal issues, as well as problems of the Wyrd variety. I also have what I call the 'relaxation zone' next to my office, where you can go and decompress." He nodded to Mrs. M and to the students.

"Oh right, one last thing." He left the room again for a short time before returning with a small box. Inside the box there were two metal rings. "These are rings made of iron and silver. The inner ring is iron and the outer ring with the celtic knotwork is silver. It should protect you from fae and various other supernatural beings you may come across. And it works as a fidget because you can spin the ring. Do be careful if you encounter fae with it, as the iron does tend to anger them unnecessarily if they do not mean you harm. Best to keep it hidden away until you need it."

He placed the box down on the table. Liam took one of the rings and Nora followed suit. Sliding it onto her thumb, the cool metal felt smooth against her skin. Liam was already spinning his around his index finger. Kimi held her hand up to show where hers rested on her middle finger.

"They are fun, aren't they?" Mr. Walker said, "Anyway, I hope you all have a good day. Stop by any time." He seemed to be in a rush, he was about to leave once again when Mrs. M cleared her throat. "Oh yes, and I would be remiss if I forgot to mention to you not to make any deals with supernatural creatures, especially not the fae." He hurried out of the room turning in the opposite direction to the way he had entered.

Mrs. M took her place in front of the whiteboard again while flattening down her skirt. "First things first, what is the main ability of a Wyrd student?"

Liam shrugged. "We can talk to each other in our heads?"

Kimi raised her hand and was called on. "The main ability of a Wyrd student is observation. We excel at seeing and noticing details that others don't. We have the gift of noticing problems, questioning situations, and coming up with solutions."

"Excellent answer, Kimi. A questioning mind is ever so important for learning. Think of yourselves as explorers or scientists, since many renowned inventors have, in fact, been Wyrd. I will be teaching you a rough history of those who have been gifted in the past and what we know about Wyrd abilities from them, but there are history texts in our extended library that it would be good for you to familiarize yourself with at some point."

"There's a library here?" Nora asked and couldn't help but be a little excited. She loved libraries. They tended to be warm and quiet, full of not only books, but art and even games.

"Of course, now Kimi will give you a tour of the East Wing...which I believe you two were calling the *Secret Wing?* A little too spot-on don't you think? Calling a secret a secret?"

Liam and Nora could not help but share a smile at the jab. They followed Kimi out of the door into the hallway that led to the fish tank full of jelly-fish and the inky creature Nora could sense watching them. Continuing down the hallway, they passed multiple doorways and one other corridor, which Nora recalled was the way back to the rest of the school.

First Kimi showed them into another classroom. It was larger and less modern-looking, but it had beanbag chairs and a couch along with tables and areas to study. There were several plants around the room and the lighting brought about a more relaxed atmosphere than most classrooms. Although Nora noted that even secret magical classrooms had the obligatory box of paper in the corner with a picture of a man with a handlebar mustache on it. There was an older girl in the room. Her dark hair was braided tightly and pinned to her head. She was sitting on the couch and reading a book, which she did not look up from when they entered.

"Hey, Maria, I'm showing the new students around," Kimi explained.

'That is painfully obvious, Kimi,' Maria sent her thoughts to all of them, *'you can see I'm busy. Did you need applause or something?'* She never turned her attention from her book, but her eyebrow twitched slightly.

Nora was amazed at how rude the girl was and how much displeasure she was able to convey through her thoughts. Oddly enough, even her thoughts had a slight hispanic accent to them, and it made Nora wonder if her thoughts sounded like her voice. Kimi and Liam had already moved on to the rest of the tour leaving Nora behind. When she hurried out after them, she was sure Maria glanced up from her book to watch her leave.

"Don't mind her," Kimi was saying while taking them to the next room. "She seems mean, but it's all an act. She's actually a really caring person underneath it all."

Chapter 6

The door was tall and wooden with intricate carvings of animals, which Nora thought might be visual representations of Aesop's Fables. She also wondered if the smaller door in the center was for decoration since a person would not fit through it. Upon turning the crystal handle, Kimi pushed into a room with a glass dome on the top of the ceiling that caused Nora to wonder how the East Wing remained secret at all. Two stories of bookshelves towered over them in the large room. The floor was carpeted in blue with the pattern of a large compass. The carpet was thick and soft beneath her shoes.

Multi-colored tomes of all shapes and sizes filled the bookshelves. Brass ladders on wheels leaned against the tall shelves, and the center of the room had long wooden tables with old desk lamps from entirely different eras.

In the center of one of the tables a black cat with a tuft of white fur on its chest snoozed in a beam of light cast down from the glass dome ceiling.

"That's Yeats, the librarian." Kimi pointed to the sleeping cat, whose ear twitched in response.

Liam snorted at the joke. "Right, a cat librarian. Are cats even allowed in a school? I'm allergic."

"No, he really is the librarian. Yeats isn't a cat exactly, he's a Cat Sith, and he knows a lot. If you can get him to tell you anything," Kimi explained while shoving her hands into her jean pockets and pulling out a cat treat. "I'm terribly sorry for bothering you," Kimi approached the cat and set a treat down next to him.

Yeats lazily opened his eyes to reveal two green orbs. He sniffed at the treat, but did not attempt to eat it. He then stretched to reveal that he was a bit longer than most cats. His sleek black fur had a bluish tinge in the sunlight. Licking one paw before yawning, he glared at Liam. 'No one is allergic to cats themselves. You're allergic to the dander caused by cat saliva when they clean themselves.' He then licked at his paw again, slowly.

The low voice floated into Nora's head. She could feel the sense of superiority oozing from each word. 'Cats can talk?!' Nora gasped.

"No way!" Liam exclaimed.

'Is it just me or do fifth-graders keep looking younger? I tire of the new recruits. It's a good thing I'm here to keep this library safe from their ignorance.' He turned around in a circle and plopped back down onto the table unceremoniously.

'I'm so sorry we've offended you,' Nora thought quickly. Now that she knew a talking cat existed, she wanted to spend every minute of every day with it. But, from her experience with cats, she realized she should not sound too eager. '*We should let you rest.*'

The cat's tail swirled back and forth, betraying its newfound interest. '*No, no. You've already woken me, and you must acquaint yourself with the library if you intend to be of any use. I believe the section of interest to you is in the right corner on the bottom. An orange book labeled,* **Lost and Found: Creatures with Sticky Fingers.**' His green eyes were almost glowing as they met Nora's.

'*How did you know about the thing Cam and I are looking for?*' Nora wondered.

But Yeats had already put his head back down, intent on ignoring the three of them. Kimi shrugged as if this was normal behavior for him. Liam let out a loud sneeze, causing the two girls to jump. Grabbing a tissue from a nearby table and handing it to Liam, Kimi gave him a sympathetic look.

Kimi said, "*we can come back here after the rest of the tour. You'll be spending a lot of time in here anyway.*"

As Kimi led them out of the room, Nora could not help but feel disappointed that she could not spend more time talking to Yeats or going through one of the coolest libraries she had ever seen. Even though she knew she'd have time there later, she didn't want to continue on the tour. Peeking back at Yeats she said, "Thanks," before they left.

Once the door was closed behind them, Liam said with a stuffy nose, "It just had to be a cat. This day just keeps getting better."

"Yeats is a Cat Sith. Like I said, not the same thing." Kimi said.

"Ok, what's that?" Liam asked, blowing his nose again.

"It's a faerie creature. He's wise, magical, and knows a lot more than us."

"Sure looks like a cat," Liam replied, grumpily.

Nora concealed the fact that she couldn't wait to go back to the library. Not only did she love cats, but this was her first real encounter with a mythological creature. There was so much she could learn from him, if she could get him to talk to her.

"I've seen that look before," Kimi said.

Nora had not even realized Kimi was watching her.

"What look?"

"You're excited about all of this, that's natural. But, you've got to be careful. The things we notice can be really dangerous. Yeats is mostly harmless, but he's still a faerie. Don't make any deals with him for anything other than food or cat toys. He can be really helpful...sometimes. But, never forget what he really is. In fact, as soon as we get back to class, you should read up on what a Cat Sith is." Kimi said matter-of-factly. She pulled her dark hair back into a bun behind her head and rolled up the sleeves of her flannel shirt.

There were two doors left at the end of the hallway. One of them was open, and through it came peaceful flute music, along with the rhythmic sound of some sort of hollow reed accompanied by moving water. Once they came around the corner, Nora could hardly believe what she was seeing. It was a rock garden, with patterns in the sand, and water moving through it, like you would see at a temple or shrine. Even though she knew it was indoors, it really felt like they were outside. Lying back in a comfortable-looking reclined chair was AJ. His eyes were closed and he was breathing slowly.

"This is Mr.Walker's relaxation room, and next door is his office. You can go to either whenever you want, but his door's closed, so I don't think he's there. He's kind of cheesy, but he actually listens and he knows a lot about magical protections and stuff. He's probably the nicest person here. Not that Mrs. M is mean or anything, she's just really... straightforward." Kimi took a step into the relaxation room and put her hand into the sand.

Nora and Liam followed suit and found the sand to be incredibly smooth. Something about letting it run between their fingers was really satisfying. Then Liam leaned back in one of the chairs and closed his eyes.

"We should be getting back to Mrs. M. She has to go over the basics with you two before we get back to regular class." Kimi didn't wait to make sure Liam was going with them. She may have assumed he knew the way back, or she just didn't want to waste any time.

While they were walking, Nora decided to ask the question that had been bothering her since Cam mentioned it. "Are you and Maria the only Wyrd seventh and eighth graders?"

Kimi stopped walking for a second. She tried to appear as though she was examining a speck on the wall where the paint was uneven. "Hmm? Oh, yeah, just us."

"I guess there just aren't that many Wyrd students each year? How many were there before you?" Nora pressed her.

Without looking back, Kimi continued walking again. "I don't know, a few. Mrs. M can answer about that better than I can."

"Well, didn't you spend time with them here, when you were in fifth and sixth grade I mean?" Nora followed closely to Kimi, and Liam had caught up. She could tell that he knew Nora was on to something and was keeping his mouth shut. Although she really wanted to talk to Liam about everything Cam and she had discussed, she wasn't sure if he was still mad at her about suggesting they not hang out for a while.

"Yeah, Mrs. M can tell you about it. Actually, I gotta get some stuff done for regular classes, just let Mrs. M know I'll see you tomorrow for buddy time." Kimi smiled awkwardly revealing silver braces and waved before turning to the other hallway.

"That was weird," Liam said more to himself than to Nora.

Nora nodded.There was too much she didn't know yet, but she was sure they were deliberately hiding something about the previous Wyrd students. Did something happen to them or was the Secret Wing newer than they thought? She had to find out more about the Secret Wing before she could even attempt to come up with theories about what was going on.

They walked back to the classroom silently. Mrs. M had arranged the room with posters stuck to the glass walls. She was writing numbers on the dry-erase board as they entered. Without turning to face them, she spoke.

"I assume the tour went well?" Without waiting for a reply, she continued. "Excellent. I'm glad you know where the important parts of the building are. There is also my office and a few other rooms that will not be of use to you. Back to the basics: there have been people gifted with what we call Wyrd throughout history. Generally the abilities become more prominent around the age of twelve. These abilities can range from noticing supernatural beings to being able to quickly come to solutions of complicated problems. Of course, a defining ability which all of us can manifest is the ability to transmit our thoughts to others with Wyrd, but many can also convey emotions to animals or speak to beings which do not share our language." Mrs. M wrote a word on the board and pointed at it. "We call it *sense* as in "sixth sense", also known as telepathy or ESP. You may have heard some of these terms before."

"We're like Marvel Superheroes!" Liam said.

"Absolutely not. We need to get that idea out of your head immediately. Having Wyrd can be advantageous, but there are many drawbacks. There are dangerous creatures that will try to take advantage of you or even just attack you for noticing them. You must never make a deal with a faerie or any supernatural creature for anything aside from actual trinkets, but it is best to discuss any sort of deal with me or Mr. Walker— or better yet, don't make them at all." Mrs. M held a wooden pointer to a poster with the picture of a little man covered in porcupine quills on it. His face was scrunched up in a grimace and he held a knife menacingly. "This is a Pukwudgie. There are some of them living in the woods next to the school. We have an arrangement with them to avoid one another, so as long as you do not stare at them or bring attention to them when you see them, they should leave you alone. They can be dangerous if you trifle with them."

Now seemed like as good a time as any to ask Mrs. M about what was bothering her. Nora raised her hand. "Mrs. M? I was just wondering why there are barely any Wyrd students? Is there normally only one or two per year?"

Mrs. M turned and glanced from Nora to Liam before sitting in a chair across from them. Nora felt a little uncomfortable being at a table with the teacher.

"There may very well be more fifth graders; it is early in the year. Generally there are three or four in each grade. But, I assume you are referring to the *incident*. Last year, there was a malicious supernatural creature. It caused many problems, and although we were able to rid the school of it, the emotional toll on the students was high. Many of them decided to move or change schools. We respected their decision, and we do not talk about it. The younger students were not involved. Please do not ask the other students about what happened or investigate it. You could bring up trauma and upset them. Are we clear?" She eyed them above her thick-framed glasses.

Liam and Nora nodded.

"Good, now if we can continue with what you absolutely need to know. Over here you will see a photo of one of the lunchroom staff. Do not look into her left eye. She is not human. We don't need to make a big thing of it." She paused, and raised an eyebrow to make sure they were paying attention. "The boiler room of the school is off limits as are the rooms on either side. There is nothing you need from those rooms." She sighed, pushing the longer side of her red hair behind her ear and peering at the clock. "We are running out of time for today. It is essential that you bring any supernatural sighting information to us before you look into it further. We will assess the danger of each situation before you get yourself involved. Even the smallest clue of something abnormal should be reported. Most of what we do here is independent study, but it will be directed by Mr. Walker and myself. Always err on the side of caution." Just as Mrs. M finished speaking, the bell rang to initiate transition to second period.

Nora was feeling a little frustrated that she did not have a chance to go back to the library and talk to Yeats or examine the book he suggested. It would be helpful to do more research on the creature stealing people's items before they searched for it during recess. By the time Nora realized she was hesitating, Liam was out the door. He had rushed off to his next class without talking to her. Now she was positive he was upset with her.

Her second class (which was her first normal class) was math, and she found her classroom easily. Generally, she enjoyed math class, but she could not help but feel like people were gawking at her and even whispering about her. She knew it had to do with the bus incident. All she could think to do was act as though she was entirely absorbed in the lesson. Unfortunately, she was not able to keep her mind on what Mrs. Stokes was teaching for very long, since Ava, who was considered one of the popular girls, dropped a note on her desk when she walked by to sharpen her pencil.

All it said was: 'Are you and Liam dating? Circle Yes/No'

Nora shoved the note into her textbook and avoided anyone's gaze for the rest of the class period. After an excruciatingly long math lesson, Nora managed to rush out of the room just before the bell rang and avoid contact with anyone. She knew her next class would go much smoother. She had art and it was mixed grades. As she made her way to the art room, she noticed the hallway was getting more and more colorful. At first the walls were painted like a rainbow going from red to purple, and then there were large murals with wizards and forests along with the dates of the classes that painted them.

One area stood out from the rest. For some reason, a wall in between two murals was simply painted white. Pausing to examine it, she could swear whenever the light hit it, there appeared to be some sort of aquatic scene with fish and perhaps sharks. It was hard for her to be certain, but she knew she had to get moving or she would be late. She liked the idea of the art room slowly invading the rest of the school and maybe the boring parts of the school were fighting back by removing some color.

CHAPTER 7

By the time Nora made it to class, students were already sitting in stools at different tables chatting to one another about summer vacation. Nora recognized Maria at one of the tables by herself and even though she knew she shouldn't draw attention to the acquaintance, for some reason her legs moved her right over to that table. She sat down a seat away from Maria and centered her gaze onto a weird sculpture someone had made from paper mache.

'*Hope you don't mind if I sit here,*' Nora sensed.

Pouring out the pencils from her case, Maria began to organize them on the table. She was sitting a little too straight to be comfortable and her long hair, even pulled back in a braid, was almost touching the stool she sat on. 'I don't own the art room,' she sensed back.

'Do you know if we're all going to be doing the same thing or are they going to separate us by grades?' Nora wondered while studying the sculpture and raising an eyebrow at its peculiar shape.

'Both, depending on what it is. You might just get a simpler version, unless you prove yourself to be advanced'. Maria finished organizing her pencils and folded her hands on the long table in front of her. *'Your eyes?'*

Nora was startled and accidentally glanced at Maria.

'What about them?'

'They are yellow, almost golden. I've never seen eyes like yours.'

Unsure how to respond, Nora shrugged. *'My mom is from Suriname.'*

'My family's from Puerto Rico. Hablas Espanol?'

Nora got that question a lot due to her dark hair and tan skin. *'No, my mom speaks Dutch.'*

Two more students whom Nora did not recognize took the other two stool seats at their table. There was plenty of space in between each of them. They were both sixth-graders. The red-headed one with freckles introduced himself as, 'Mac,' and the girl in overalls with pigtails, 'Steph'.

Well after class should have started, the art teacher rushed into the room. Her hair was a flurry of frizz around her head and a long, flowing smock floated after her as she moved. Her arms were full of clay blocks and tools. "I'm so sorry kids, I couldn't find my cart and I wanted to make sure we got started working with clay today." As she rushed around the room plopping lumps of clay on each table, she dropped a variety of tools to the floor.

After a fun and very messy art class, Nora was feeling much better about everything. No one asked her about what happened on the school bus, since they likely didn't know or care. Mac had a lot of trouble shaping anything out of clay that wasn't a lumpy monster with a big nose, which looked nothing like the pots they were supposed to be starting with and caused a tremendous amount of laughter to erupt from Steph whenever she glimpsed it. Nora even saw Maria crack a smile at the corner of her mouth while silently constructing the perfect bowl.

But, right as class ended, while students were cleaning up their clay, Maria sensed to Nora, '*Your friend, is he really Wyrd?*'

Nora put her clay on the drying rack and turned around to view Maria. She could see there was something troubling her by the pained expression on her face.

'*Why?*' Nora began to fidget with the ring Mr. Walker had given her. She spun the iron loop inside the silver ring.

'*When two people are close, one of them probably isn't. Just the way it is, and he seems less likely.*' Maria sensed while gathering up all of her belongings and placing them neatly into different pockets of her backpack.

'*OK, so what if he isn't.*' It was hard for her not to get defensive when it came to Liam.

'*You need to tell him the truth. It's just better that way.*'

Nora clenched her jaw. Maria didn't know them or the situation. '*He already told me he wouldn't give up knowing all of it.*'

Maria got up and peered down at Nora. Eighth graders were like giants in comparison to the younger students. '*You need to tell him. It's for his own good.*'

'*He's my best friend.*'

'*Then do the right thing.*' Maria turned abruptly and her long ponytail trailing behind her as she left the classroom.

Even though she wanted to yell after Maria that it was none of her business and to stay out of it, she knew it wouldn't do any good. She would just look like a crazy person yelling to a mostly empty classroom after a girl who hadn't actually spoken more than a word to her. Making up her mind that Maria was a rude know-it-all, she decided not to read too much into the conversation.

Despite the fact that she was flustered after the encounter, Nora was proud of herself for finding her way to her locker and the lunchroom without any trouble. She immediately scanned the room for Liam's bright blue t-shirt, but he was nowhere to be seen. Shrugging, she pulled out her lunch bag and sat at the same table they had the day before. Other students began to fill in and chat with their friends, and she began to feel a little out of place. Where could Liam be? Would she have to eat lunch alone?

Just then a kid she didn't recognize took a seat across from her. Even though he was short for his age, around her height, she could tell he was one of the older kids from a small amount of facial hair forming above his lip. There was something else that was off about him, but Nora couldn't quite figure it out.

"Yo, you got slime?" He pulled several plastic zipper bags filled with the dark gunk Nora had seen the other kids playing with out of his backpack .

"Uh, no," she replied, "Are you supposed to be in this lunch?"

"Shh, it's cool. It's $3 for one or $5 for two. People call me, 'Fresh,' and I'm the only one who's got the real stuff. Everyone else has knockoffs." He stopped and squinted at Nora's eyes. "Wait, you in those special ed classes, in the East Wing? You want a free sample?"

Unsure how Fresh knew she was going to the Secret Wing and also feeling a bit irritated by whatever he was implying, she was about to reply indignantly when the lunchroom monitor walked by. Fresh suddenly went very still, but she continued past them. Shoving all of the bags back into his backpack, he slung it over his shoulder and nodded at Nora before sliding over to another table to discuss his wares.

She saw a few fifth-graders paying Fresh for some slime. They were already playing with it before lunch ended, but Fresh was long gone. Nora had almost finished her sandwich when a boy stood up and announced. "Look, I made Nora and Liam!" He held up toothpicks with fruit on the ends and started smashing them together while making kissing noises.

Nora could feel her face burning. The students at the table, who happened to be the same ones who had just purchased slime, laughed loudly. Before she could react the lunch monitor grabbed the kid by his arm and pulled him out of his seat. One of her eyes was a glossy, light blue and the other was a dark brown, almost red. Instantly, Nora knew it was the one lunch staff she should not be staring at, but was uncertain as to which eye was the peculiar one.

"No one makes a mess in my lunchroom. You're cleaning the whole room during recess!" she said in a gravelly voice.

The other students went silent, and he slumped his head in reply. Just then the bell rang to release them and Nora remembered she was supposed to meet Cam outside of the lunchroom so they could investigate the objects going missing. As she turned the corner she almost ran into him. Cam's braids flew over his eyes as he stopped short. He put out a hand to steady Nora, but she did not take it.

'*You OK?*' he sensed.

Since there was nothing she could do about the fact that her face was still flushed, she simply shrugged and responded. '*Yeah, where do we start?*'

Cam continued down the hallway towards the gymnasium. The lights were on but there wasn't a class in it. '*There were a lot of gym socks and totally random stuff going missing around here, so I think we should check the locker rooms for any clues. There's a storage area under the bleachers that something could definitely hide in.'* Upon stepping into the gymnasium, his shoes squeaked on the polished floor.

The doors to the locker rooms were only accessible from inside the gymnasium. After noisily walking to the far side of the gymnasium, they grabbed the metal handles to their respective doors and pulled them open. The stale smell of unused showers full of mildew poured out.

'Remember, if you see any signs of something supernatural, don't go near it. Just act like you didn't notice and meet me back here.' Cam sensed before the locker room door swung shut behind him.

It was eerie being in a locker room by herself. Nora kept feeling like one of the stall doors would pop open at any minute. The room was made of cement which had been painted yellow and the floors were tile with drains. Rows of lockers lined the walls, some hanging open with dust collecting in them. Heat sizzled through the vents making the smell worse and giving the air an oppressive thickness. She held her thumb with the ring on it in her fist, hoping that the metals would protect her like Mr. Walker had explained. Then she began walking down the line of lockers and opening each one to find them entirely empty, not even a forgotten pen. Perhaps the custodians did a very thorough job before the summer.

She continued to the showers, which had their own stalls. Again, there was nothing out of the ordinary. The entire locker room was incredibly clean, even though the scent of the room suggested otherwise. Trusting her instincts, she shoved open the frosted glass window at the end of the locker room to let some fresh air in. Beside the window, there was a worn out window-jam made out of a bunch of rulers taped together. By the looks of it, the window jam was used often. As she headed back to the gymnasium, she saw Cam outside waiting for her.

"Nothing in there," Nora said.

"Nothing at all?" Cam asked.

Nora simply shook her head.

"Yeah, same with the other one. I've never seen them so clean before. Not even a rolled up sock shoved behind the lockers or a gum wrapper." Cam squinted his eyes. His hands rested on his hips over his basketball jersey as he thought back to his memory of the locker room.

"We haven't had to use the locker rooms yet, maybe it's just clean from the summer?" Nora wondered.

Cam shrugged and took squeaky steps over to the bleachers. One set had been pulled out and the others were still pushed against the wall. Motioning for Nora to follow him, Cam went under the bleachers that had been pulled out. They did not have to duck to walk under the tallest portion. In the floor was a trap door with a metal ring to pull it up.

While taking a thin, metal flashlight out of his pocket, Cam sensed to Nora, '*This is where they keep the extra chairs and stuff. I think it would be a good place to hide. I'm going to open it, can you shine the flashlight in? If we see anything, we'll just close it right away.*'

Nora took the flashlight and readied herself for the trap door to open. As she spun the metal ring, her imagination was filled with all kinds of monsters leaping out at her once the door opened. She pictured a furry beast with horns and claws flinging itself at them and her ring magically repelling it like a force field.

As soon as Cam lifted it, Nora realized she didn't know how the flashlight worked. She thought there was a button and then found out she had to twist it. With an amused expression on his face, Cam watched Nora fiddle with the flashlight before turning it on. Dust poured out of the small space and floated in the small beam of light. They covered their faces as best they could and peered inside. There were dozens of folding chairs sitting on top of one another, undisturbed. Nora shifted the light to the floor and to the back of the space, there was nothing out of the ordinary.

Soon after Cam closed the floor door, they heard noisy footsteps in the gymnasium. They both froze in place under the bleachers. Cam's eyes went wide. It was then that Nora felt her nose itching and a sneeze coming on from the dust.

'*Cam, I think I'm going to sneeze!*'

'*Don't do it!*'

Nora frantically tried to cover her nose and then her whole face in her sleeves. The footsteps continued across the gymnasium to the other side and then they heard a door close just as Cam let out an enormous sneeze himself. Nora was so startled by it that she almost thought she had sneezed as well. She smiled at Cam who was grinning back at her and they both began to laugh the kind of laugh that bubbles out of you with relief after holding back.

'*Let's get out of here,*' Cam thought.

The two of them quickly shuffled across the gym and back to the exit.

"Well, that was a bust," Cam said as soon as they were outside in the hallway by themselves, "kind of fun though."

"Yeah, I've got some books to look through later on today to try to figure out what it is," Nora said.

"Cool. I should get going, my lunch is almost over. Same time tomorrow? I know where we should look next."

When Nora nodded, they separated and headed to their respective locations. Nora had never snuck around a school or skipped recess before. She felt like a spy or secret agent or something, and it was exhilarating. She just wished Liam could have been there, sneezing with them.

CHAPTER 8

Later that day, Nora was happy to discover she had a free period which allowed her to go to the Secret Wing to do some research. She rushed down the hall, completely ignoring any side eye from other students as to her enthusiasm. She found the library quickly and went straight to the corner Yeats had pointed out. She didn't see the cat anywhere when she entered. Her feet sunk into the plush carpet and the sun shone in, even warmer than earlier, but at a different angle.

The smaller shelf in the back contained quite a few larger books, but the section was easy enough to find. Yeats had described it as an orange book in the right corner called "Lost and Found: Creatures with Sticky Fingers." Sliding her hand across the binding of the books, she stopped as soon as she came to a thick orange one. She knew immediately that it was what she was looking for. There was even a drawing of a sock on the cover.

On pulling it out, she sat on the floor with the book on her lap and flipped it open to the index. Just then a black streak leapt down from the shelf nearby and landed heavily on the book. Nora started and gasped. Yeats squinted his eyes, looking pleased with himself.

'*What took you so long?*' he asked.

'*I have classes, this is school.*' Nora pointed out.

'*Oh, who cares about all of that.*' Yeats shoved the book to the floor with his body and curled up in Nora's lap in its stead. His voice, which she heard in her head, was exactly how she would picture it—not high pitched like a cat, but not too low either. It was smooth and calming, like a jazz singer with a hint of what she could only describe as mischief. '*Take that ring off, I don't want to get sick.*'

Nora had almost forgotten about the ring on her thumb and how Mr. Walker had told them it might annoy some faerie creatures, like Yeats. She quickly slid it into her backpack, so as not to insult him. It was an odd experience to have an intelligent, talking cat in her lap. It almost made her doubt petting him, but she couldn't help herself and Yeats soon purred in response.

'*Well, go on, let's see what we find.*' He motioned his paw to the book.

Nora scanned the index, but soon realized she did not know what any of the creatures were, and would be better off flipping through. Each page had a rendering of a creature along with a detailed description, much like the encyclopedia she had flipped through in the glass classroom. There was a whole section on faeries that may take small objects: Brownies, Hobgoblins, Gnomes, Knockers, and as she skimmed through, Yeats had something to say about each one.

'*Nope, they're in houses, not schools. They wouldn't steal random objects. They're generally helpful.*' He continued this way until they had flipped through most of the faerie creatures.

'*Did Cam tell you the details?*' Nora asked.

Yeats ignored her question. '*Scratch my cheek, human girl.*'

Nora obliged but sent back, '*My name is **Nora**.*'

Yeats rolled onto his back and put his paws in the air. '*Well, Noh-rah, I think we've ruled out the fae. Let's start with spirits, or maybe it's a sentient creature made of junk.*'

It suddenly dawned on Nora that Yeats had asked others for favors in the past for assistance. She hoped she did not unwittingly make some sort of deal with him. '*Why are you helping me?*'

'*Don't look a gift horse in the mouth.*' He pawed at her hand playfully.

'*What does that even mean?*' Nora wondered.

'*You can tell how old a horse is by its teeth. It's being ungrateful, because someone gifted you a horse, and now you're going to see how good it is.*'

'*What if I don't want a horse? Horses are expensive and a lot of work, especially an old one,*' Nora pointed out.

'*You're going to do well here. Let's just say I'm bored, and I like your pets.*' He yawned and rolled to his feet. Sitting on the floor next to the book, he used his front paw to flip to a page with the drawing of a pile of clothes, pens, toys, and other small objects. The pile of clothing had what appeared to be a coin for one eye, a six-sided die for another, and a sock for a nose. It could have been a weird art project, except for the description which explained how a pile of unwanted objects could form together and become a moving creature.

'*You think this is what we're looking for?*' Nora sensed while pointing at the drawing.

'*How should I know?*'

'*I think it must be! It doesn't seem too dangerous. It's just picking up garbage that people leave behind.*' Nora read the description more thoroughly, '*although, I guess it could get pretty big at a school like this. It says here that they often fall apart on their own. Do we have any other books with more details on this thing?*'

Yeats scanned the bookshelves with his iridescent cat eyes. '*You can't see the forest for the trees.*'

'*Do you always talk in proverbs?*'

'*I live in a library, my dear Noh-rah. If you focus too much on one solution, you will close your mind to possibilities and miss something important.*' He leapt from the floor onto a shelf and wove through a ladder with ease to trot across a bookshelf. It was hard not to admire his stealth. '*But, why bother listening to me? I'm just a cat.*'

'*You're not just a cat though,*' Nora reminded herself as she sent it.

'*Bring sashimi next time. Salmon.*' And with that Yeats somehow vanished into the back of a bookshelf.

Closing the book and returning it to the shelf, Nora knew she had to go back to her regular classes and continue out the rest of her day. She hoped she would run into Liam .She had a lot to tell him, even if he was still angry with her. Unable to pay any attention to her last classes, the rest of the day seemed to drag on forever. She didn't catch Liam in the hallway, so she would have to tell him about everything on the bus ride home. Even if they couldn't sit next to one another anymore, she could always sense to him, and she didn't mind if AJ eavesdropped.

To her surprise, when she got on the bus to go home, Liam was nowhere to be seen. Skip had arranged a seating chart which he taped to the front seat. She saw Liam's name on the front seat right next to Skip and immediately felt sorry for him. Upon finding her own seat she recognized the girl she was sitting next to as the sixth-grader they had talked to the day before. Unfortunately, she wasn't sure of her name and felt uncomfortable asking at this point. She was silently kicking herself for not checking the girl's name on the seating chart when she realized AJ was behind her.

'Liam's got detention,' AJ sensed, *'for causing a disturbance on the bus.'*

'That's ridiculous!' Nora almost yelled out loud.

'Skip wanted to give you one too, but Liam insisted you had nothing to do with it, and the Vice Principal believed him. I guess Liam had a bunch of detentions on his record and you just had straight A's.' AJ slid into his seat awkwardly as another student sat next to him. It was a fifth grader who also did not seem too happy about sitting next to AJ. It was obvious that AJ's eccentricities along with the stories about him made kids uncomfortable.

'He had a few detentions, but those really weren't his fault. I mean, they were for stupid reasons.' Nora felt herself growing defensive. Most of the detentions Liam had received were due to them investigating the strange things they had seen. He had stayed out at recess too long once because they were hearing noises, he was caught searching through a teacher's desk for a bizarre confiscated item which disappeared, and he was always getting into trouble for drawing in his notebook instead of doing classwork. Maybe she had made his life worse for getting him involved with the supernatural occurrences she was seeing. He never would have gotten into trouble if it weren't for her.

'Just telling you what I heard.'

It was then that Nora realized the girl next to her had asked her a question and was waiting for a response.

"What?" Nora asked.

The girl's dirty-blond hair was pulled back so tightly into a ponytail, that she almost looked bald from the front. Everything from her backpack to her bright white sneakers were impeccably clean. "I was just saying the assigned seating isn't a big deal, a lot of bus drivers do that anyway. It's not your fault."

"Thanks," Nora said, but doubted the other students on the bus felt that way.

"And, we all know Liam is just…well you know. He's always getting into trouble."

Nora was growing angry. Liam wasn't a bad kid, he just always ended up in the wrong place at the wrong time. It wasn't his fault. Unsure if she would start to yell at the girl if the conversation continued, Nora just nodded and shifted her attention out the window.

"Are the two of you dating, though? That's what everyone's saying." She continued.

Realizing that the girl was only being nice to her in order to get the first-hand gossip, Nora gritted her teeth together. "No, we're just friends."

"Is he dating someone else then?" She kept going.

"No," Nora said a little too loudly. "Why is everyone making such a big deal out of this? We just started fifth grade?!"

The girl shrugged, obviously a little annoyed by Nora's outburst. "I knew kids who were dating in fourth grade, and you two hang out together all the time." She pulled her phone out of her backpack and began texting without caring if Nora could see what she was typing.

It said, "Stuck in assigned seating thanks to those smooching fifth-graders."

Nora decided to go back to gazing out the window and organizing all of her thoughts about what had happened that day. This way she could call Liam and give him a full account once he got home. After getting him into this mess, she owed it to him to make sure he knew as much as she did. Besides, talking with Liam always helped her figure out problems.

Eventually, the bus screeched to a halt at her stop. When she walked by Skip, his face was wrinkled into a particularly angry grimace, which seemed to be more common with him now. He was always gruff, but Nora never remembered him being mean. Something had changed to make him always ready to snap, and whatever it was, Nora hoped it would get better. Holding the rail, she shuffled down the steps and made her way to her house. Momma G was probably asleep and her sister would be home soon.

She thought about leaving a message for Liam online, but wasn't sure if he'd check. Writing him a note and leaving it at his house seemed like a lot of work, so she made up her mind to call him. But later that evening, when she called his house, his dad picked up and told her that Liam was grounded and was not allowed to talk on the phone or go on the computer. Not wanting to get him into more trouble, she decided not to go to his house and try to sneak him a note instead. She would be able to talk to him on the bus the next day, and they had several classes together.

Unfortunately for Nora, Liam was not on the school bus again in the morning. They didn't have class together in the Secret Wing until the end of the day, so if he wasn't home sick, they'd have to sense to one another in Science class and try not to get caught zoning out.

The day began with what she was most dreading—homeroom. The group of popular girls sat together in the same seats as before, playing with their dark slime. The ringleader of the group, Jess, sat in the center next to another sixth-grader and Penelope, whom Nora had once been friendly with, was to her left. The rest of the class had split off into different corners. Nora expected to hear them gossiping about her and Liam or to confront her, but before the teacher, Mrs. Stokes, could even make the announcements, Penelope grabbed Jess by the hair and pulled her to the ground.

Chairs slid back, students gathered around. The two girls rolled over each other, hitting and screaming. The other girls at the table seemed to be rooting for either Penelope or Jess depending on who appeared to be winning. Meanwhile, the incensed teacher was in the process of dispersing the students and separating the two girls. Having remained in her seat, Nora was able to see the girls between the legs of the other students. They had crazed expressions on their faces, like nothing she had ever seen. They grabbed at one another, shoving faces into the floor and tugging on hair or loose clothing to try to get a leg up on the other one. Something wasn't right, but she didn't have time to ponder it. The fight ended as quickly as it had started.

Mrs. Stokes called for the vice principal to collect both the girls. They glared at one another. Penelope's arms were folded across her chest and Jess had her hands on her hips. After telling the rest of the students to remain in their seats quietly, Mrs. Stokes escorted the girls into the hallway, but the door remained open. Everyone in the classroom went quiet, listening to the conversation in the hall.

"What do you two think you were doing?!" Mrs. Stokes nearly yelled at them while they waited outside the door.

"She took my slime," Penelope whined.

"I did not!" Jess screamed.

"The slime again? I'm sick of this stuff. We need to ban it from school. Give it to me, I'm confiscating it." Mrs. Stokes said. "You will both stand here silently until the Vice Principal arrives. Ah, there he is."

The rest of homeroom was less eventful, but Nora was selfishly glad the fight had drawn attention away from her. Judging by the whispers during the rest of homeroom, the school would be buzzing about the fight in a matter of minutes. Finding it odd that Penelope, whom she always knew to be shy, would attack anyone, let alone a sixth-grader, Nora made a mental note to tell Liam about it once they had class together.

Her next class seemed to drag on forever. She heard a few kids talking about the fight and asking if anyone saw it, but Nora kept her mouth shut. Science couldn't come soon enough. When the bell rang Nora practically leapt from her seat.

On entering the Science room, Nora automatically walked over to the table she and Liam had shared the previous day. But, to her surprise, after she sat down, she saw Liam sitting in the back with another kid and chatting to him in the back of the room. After watching him for a while, she realized he purposely wasn't returning eye contact. Eventually another girl, Mia, whom Nora had several classes with, sat next to her and smiled at the fact that they had the same color notebook.

When the Science teacher walked into the room and began the lesson, Nora had come to the conclusion that Liam was mad at her. She wanted to sense to him, but he actually seemed to be paying attention to the lesson for once, and he could probably use the participation grade. Maybe he was done with all of the Wyrd stuff? It did seem like he was better off without it, since he wouldn't be getting in trouble all of the time. Had Maria been right when she told Nora to tell the truth to Liam? It didn't matter, she couldn't help but want to talk to her best friend. She felt hurt that he was ignoring her and ashamed of not only getting him involved with everything but wanting to keep him involved even if it wasn't in his best interest.

It was a relief when the Science teacher took out the microscopes and the students began examining different slides. Everyone loved microscope days, and they even got to draw what they saw. As she switched through the slides of hair follicles and plant cells, Nora was able to pull her mind away from Liam and her guilt towards him. It helped that her lab partner was easy to work with.

CHAPTER 9

When the bell rang, Liam made a beeline for the door, removing any hope that he might not be mad at her. It was going to be a lonely lunch, but at least she and Cam were going to do some more exploring. She decided she'd go to the Secret Wing and eat her lunch there. Even though she didn't have any fish for Yeats, she could still search through the library a bit to find out more information on the junk creatures.

After grabbing her lunch from her locker, she happened to see Cam on the other side of the hallway by his locker. Since he was by himself, she put herself in front of the trophy case nearby and pretended to be reading the names on them.

'I think the creature we're looking for might be the junk itself. It all just gathers together and can get really big and move around and stuff.' She sensed to Cam.

Cam hadn't noticed her at first. He closed his locker and went to examine the trophies also. *'Wow, that's crazy. Thanks for looking into it. I thought maybe it was a faerie or something.'*

Nora shook her head. *'No, Yeats didn't think it was one, and he seems to know a lot about faeries. Anyway, this thing might just fall back apart on its own.'*

'Ok, what happens if it doesn't? And what causes it?' Cam pulled the books he was carrying up to his chest and glanced down the hallway.

'It could be dangerous if it gets big and starts looking for bigger objects to add to it. I don't know why it formed. I didn't have time to find another book with more info. Do you still think we should try to find it?' Nora was watching Cam's reflection in the glass. His eyes were squinted as if he were thinking it through.

'I dunno, maybe we should investigate it...'

Just then, an older girl with dark makeup around her eyes and colorfully-dyed hair walked up to Cam. "Who's this, you got a new girlfriend?" the girl asked loudly.

Several students passing by stopped to glance.

"Didn't know you were into fifth-graders," she continued.

"What?" Cam was taken back, "Come on, Tracy. I'm not."

"Oh, then why did I see her staring at you in the glass?" Tracy asked while grinning menacingly at Nora.

Nora was flabbergasted. Why was everyone obsessed with dating here? This was exactly why most middle schools didn't have fifth grade up through eighth. It was also why Wyrd students had to be careful not to be seen together without a valid explanation.

"Look, I'm sorry if you have a crush on me, but I just met you," Cam said to Nora.

Nora's face wasn't flushed this time, she could feel herself going pale and there was a cold sweat dripping down her back. She wanted to run far away.

"Guess you can stop staring at him and following him around then," Tracy said, covering her mouth while she pretended to laugh.

By this point several students had stopped to watch the confrontation.

'I'm really sorry,' Cam sensed to Nora.

"Wait, aren't you that girl who got in trouble for making out with her boyfriend on the bus? Wow, you move fast!" While Tracy said these words, Kimi shoved her way through the crowd and grabbed Nora by the hand.

"There you are!" Kimi yelled over Tracy. "It's buddy lunch today, I've been looking all over for you! Did you get lost?" It seemed as though her words were loud enough to make it so only Cam and Nora had heard Tracy's last remark.

'Just say you were going to ask Cam for directions.' Kim sensed.

"Uh, yeah. I was going to ask him where the lunch room was and..." Nora started.

"And a bunch of uppity sixth-graders decided to give you a hard time instead. Shame on all of you. You should remember how hard it was to be new here. Come on, let's go to lunch." Kimi dragged Nora along with her and stuck out her tongue at the onlookers who were filing out to their classes.

'I really am sorry,' Cam sensed again, before they were out of sight.

'You have to be more careful!' Kimi sensed somehow emphasizing each word.

'*I know, thanks for that. I didn't know what to do, it was just so embarrassing.*' Nora buried her face in her hands.

"It's OK," Kimi said out loud. "Just be more careful from now on."

Nora nodded and followed Kimi into the lunchroom. True to her word, fifth-graders were all sitting with their seventh-grade buddies and having awkward conversations or simply eating together. Liam was sitting with a seventh-grade boy that Nora didn't recognize, but the two of them were both laughing about something. It made Nora smile.

The lunchroom was louder and more packed than usual, since there were twice as many students. So far, there had been enough space for Nora to sit at her own table during lunch, but now they had to cram into a corner at the edge of the room with other students nearby.

"How are your classes going?" Kimi asked, but she was staring out the window and absent mindedly twirling the blue braid she had clipped to her dark hair.

"Fine," Nora replied automatically.

'*Maria said you're in her art class,*' Kimi sensed. She shifted her bracelets on her arm, and Nora realized she was trying to appear distracted and uninterested in case anyone noticed them.

'*Yeah,*' Nora couldn't help herself. She was still mad at Maria for what she had said about Liam and the way she said it. '*I know you said she's not that bad, but she was really kind of rude.*'

Kimi smiled without showing her teeth and pulled out her sandwich, breaking it into small chunks the way people with braces do. '*Yeah, she can be, I guess. But, she probably has your best interest at heart.*'

'*Did she tell you about it?*' Nora wondered.

'*It's none of my business,*' Kimi said, '*but she may have mentioned it. Look, Maria has good reason to say that to you. The same thing happened to her and her brother.*'

Nora was shocked. She hadn't thought of another student going through what she was dealing with when it came to Liam. Why hadn't Maria just told her that in the first place? Nora would have listened.

'*Although, I don't know why we're all assuming you're the one that caused Liam to become Wyrd. It could be the other way around.*' Kimi suggested.

That thought hadn't occurred to Nora. Mrs. M. had told Nora that she was the one who was Wyrd, but what if she had told Liam the same thing? What if they didn't know which of the two of them was Wyrd? How would they? She tried to think back to the first time she saw or heard something supernatural, and realized that Liam was always present. He always said that she pointed it out to him, but what if she only perceived those things because he was there?

Realizing she had disturbed Nora, Kimi sat quietly eating her lunch and gazing out the window. Another seventh-grader who was wearing a shirt with an anime character on it waved to Kimi and she nodded in response.

"Lunch is almost over, I'm going to go hang with my friends, if that's cool?" Kimi said.

Nora nodded. She was still deep in thought and barely noticed Kimi walk away. Would she want to go back to a normal life, not knowing anything about the Wyrd? Absolutely not. Nothing could make her want to go back to ignorance of all the Wyrd things going on around them. This newfound power gave her the ability to help people, and Liam could too. Now, she knew exactly how he felt about the situation, and she regretted ever even thinking he would want to forget about all of it. It was his choice, just as much as it was hers, and she was positive he felt the same way. Standing up, she knew she had to find Liam and talk to him immediately.

The bell rang and students began to shuffle out to their classes. She got caught up in the sea of seventh graders who were a great deal taller and hard to see around. Hoping to catch Liam outside during recess, Nora hurried outside without bothering to put her backpack in her locker. The pine trees were tall and many had lost their lower branches, making it easy to see around their naked trunks. The ground was perpetually covered in pine-needles, keeping anything else from growing. Scanning the playground, she felt a rush of urgency when she saw Liam standing by himself near the boarded walkways that lead into the woods with his backpack on as well.

She ran over to Liam and blurted out, "I'm sorry!"

Liam smiled and scratched his head. "For what?"

"For what I said before. You were right, we're best friends. I don't care what people think!" Nora said loudly enough that any nearby student would be able to hear. "I have so much to tell you, please don't be mad at me anymore."

After a moment, Liam let out a guffaw. "Mad at you? I thought you were mad at me. I was trying to give you space like you told me to!"

Both Nora and Liam broke out laughing before Liam began walking further into the woods. They followed the boardwalk pathways that looped through the sparse trees. The on-duty teachers stood like prison-guards, spaced to be able to see students no matter which part of the playground or walkway they were on. Eventually Liam sat down on the edge of a platform and Nora joined him. Pulling out his notebook, he flipped through several pages. Nora was relieved that Liam could go on as if nothing had happened between them.

"Something's up with the bus drivers. It's not just Skip. The other drivers are acting really mean too and a bunch of them quit. I've been talking to AJ, and he's been keeping an eye on Skip. He thinks there's something supernatural and we should probably check out places they all go to, like the bus yard, but I don't know how we'll get there. It's near the marshes at the edge of town." Liam held up his cartoonish drawings of bus drivers angrily yelling at students. He then showed Nora a drawing of a toilet with a creepy-looking girl's head sticking out of it. Her hair was stringy and over her face like something out of a horror-movie.

"What is that?" Nora exclaimed.

"AJ, I mean that's not AJ. I meant to say that AJ is actually really cool. Back when he was in fourth grade, he realized he was Wyrd, which is crazy early for most kids. Like, he figured out way more than we did. He knew there were supernatural creatures around and he found out about a ghost in the bathroom. It's kind of a common story, dead girl in the third stall. Well, it's not a girl. It's a spirit that uses stories to scare people and feeds on their fear. Do you remember something about a ghost in the bathroom when we were in 3rd grade?" Liam erased and rewrote a few of his notes while he was talking. He often noticed mistakes when he was showing his notebook to Nora.

Thinking back, Nora had a vague memory about a ghost in the boys bathroom, but she just thought the older kids were trying to scare the younger ones since it was around Halloween when she heard about it. Since the older kids made a Haunted Hallway for the younger ones to walk through, she assumed it was part of their theme at the time. She nodded.

Liam went on. "It was really scaring the first graders and some of them were wetting themselves to avoid the bathroom, so AJ decided he had to do something about it. He figured out a way to get rid of it with charms and herbs like sage and stuff. And it actually worked! Too bad the thing didn't go without trying to drag him into the toilet first." Liam turned to the page he had drawn of kids walking into the bathroom to find AJ half in the toilet.

"AJ Splunker Toilet Dunker," Nora said while shaking her head. She immediately felt bad for ever even wondering about AJ and his odd habits.

"Yeah, it really kind of sucks. He did something awesome and everyone just makes fun of him for it. I guess that's why the Wyrd teachers and kids keep saying we have to be careful." He closed his notebook and took a deep breath before looking in Nora's direction. "What did you want to tell me?"

"Right," Nora could hardly figure out where to start. She was still caught up in the story about AJ and was even more upset by the way other students treated him. But, with Liam waiting patiently for her to fill him in, she had to put her remorse for AJ aside. "Cam and I have been looking for a creature that may be made up of random missing junk, like socks and pens. Also, something happened with the older Wyrd kids that no one is talking about and I'm pretty sure one of them was Maria's brother." Nora thought it would take longer for her to explain everything, and then wondered if maybe it wasn't as exciting as she thought it was.

But, when Liam's eyes lit up, she couldn't help but smile. He flipped to a new page in his notebook and wanted Nora to give him all of the details of everything that had happened. She told him all about Cam and her exploring the locker rooms, Yeats showing her the books, and Maria in art class. She was able to convey that Maria had been standoffish and rude without giving him the exact details of what she said. She then went on to tell him about the awkward encounter she had with Cam that day and how Kimi had rescued her. Liam had jotted down notes about the locker rooms and was still attempting to draw Yeats in the library. Nora hoped he wouldn't need to add the embarrassing situation with Cam into the notebook.

"You're running out of pages," Nora noticed, "We should probably label each of your notebooks, maybe color code them, and put them all somewhere safe. Maybe we can lock them up somewhere?"

"I didn't even think about it," Liam said, "Everyone always thinks I'm just writing fiction stories and drawing goofy pictures, so I figured it wouldn't matter where I put them. Hide in plain sight. But, we may want to reference them later, and if there are supernatural creatures around, we should definitely look into that." Liam stopped shading the cat and watched the other students walking by them on the boardwalk. It was two girls gossiping about the fight that had happened in the morning. "Even without the Secret Wing, our school is pretty different from other middle schools."

"Yeah," Nora agreed.

"I'm glad we're in this together," Liam said without turning to Nora.

'*Me too,*' she sensed back.

They bumped knuckles.

Then Liam slumped a bit and shuffled his feet uncomfortably. "There's just one more thing I didn't get to tell you." He paused as if thinking about how to word it, but then gave up. "My mom is insisting on driving me to school for a while. I told her how mean the bus driver is, and she decided we'd all be better off if I wasn't on the bus for a bit."

Knowing how much Liam cared for his mom and how protective she was of him was endearing to Nora. But, she knew it was embarrassing for Liam to admit. He used to run up to her when he got off the bus each day and yell about how much he missed her. Sometime in fourth grade, he had toned it down and now she no longer met him at his bus stop.

"I guess AJ and I will have to suffer without you."

"You mean the two of you will have to collect evidence without me. Until we can find a way to the bus depot, the buses are all we got. AJ thinks we should check the seats and floor and maybe see if there's something up by the driver's seat? I don't know how we'll be able to do that though."

While Liam was talking, Nora's eyes focused and unfocused on an object that was on the ground ahead of them. It was sticking up out of the pine-needles and almost looked like one of them, but it was longer and a different color. "Hey, what's that?" She finally said after watching it for a full minute.

Liam shrugged. He leapt off the platform, even though it was barely raised from the ground, and landed beside the object. Nora stepped down to join him in the pine-needles. Carefully, he brushed the pine needles away and used two fingers to lift a long, white-tipped quill. Upon lifting it, they discovered it was almost as long as Liam's forearm, much longer than a porcupine quill.

"Pukwudgie!" Both Liam and Nora said at the same time, remembering the picture of the spiny creature with the ugly, wrinkly face that Mrs. M had shown them.

"There's another one over there!" Nora pointed out.

Liam followed her gaze and rushed over to it. He then pointed at another one further up ahead. There was a whole trail of them beneath the pine-needles. "We could probably follow this to one of them or their nests. I wonder if they molt and that's why there's so many?"

"Hopefully it didn't get in a fight or injured," Nora pointed out, "But, Mrs. M said there's an agreement. We're supposed to leave them alone and they'll leave us alone. Also, maybe we should read up on what they are before we encounter one."

Although those were very good points, Liam and Nora both knew they would not follow her advice.

"Maybe we should just see where the quills are going and stop when we get there. If there's blood or something, we'd know it's in trouble. Either way, we can just turn around and go back the way we came once the trail ends or if we see anything." Liam's argument also seemed level-headed.

Nora knew that both of them were too excited about the idea of seeing one of the creatures to simply ignore the quills entirely. So, they began to follow them. The quills looped under and around the platforms. Some were far from others or so buried in the pine needles that it took a while to find them. Just as they found the last one, the bell rang and recess was over. The teachers were blowing their whistles and waving the students back inside. They did not have to rush though, because the final quill had led them right up to the side of the building.

CHAPTER 10

For their last class that day, Liam and Nora were in the Secret Wing. They had expected more lessons with Mrs. M, but she explained she was very busy and the library was full of books for them to look at. She stressed that they should talk to her about any projects they might be working on and their plans for how to go about completing their work. When they brought up the junk monster and the school buses, Mrs. M shrugged them off saying that the older students had class with her earlier in the day and could keep her updated on those. Since Mrs. M had told Nora not to investigate what had happened to the Wyrd students last year, that only left the quills they had found and they probably weren't supposed to be following the Pukwudgie's quills in the first place.

After a short silence, Mrs. M shooed them off to the library and was on her way down the hall, her high heels clicking and her elaborate purple skirt twirling behind her. It was obvious that she was in a hurry to get somewhere. Nora and Liam had plenty to look into, but when they opened the door to the library, they were both dumbstruck by the amount of resources that lay before them.

"Have you ever used cards to look up where a book is?" Nora asked Liam, motioning to the Dewey Decimal cards in wooden drawers.

"Uh, no. There's no computers in here?" Liam glanced around the room. "I guess the laptops are in the classroom." Just then, Liam stopped and his face contorted. He threw his hands up in the air and let out a big sneeze.

'Do not get your snot all over my library, you disgusting boy.' Yeats was suddenly sitting on a table beside them. His dark fur contrasted with the multicolored books around them.

'I'm only sneezing because of you!' Liam sensed.

Yeats lifted his head smugly. *'I suppose you won't be needing my help then.'*

'No! We do. He didn't mean anything by it. Can you help us find books on Pukwudgies?' Nora asked.

'I suppose,' Yeats stepped leisurely to the edge of the table and pointed his paw. *'There's Native American creatures towards the middle top, that whole 'J' section. Did you bring sashimi?'*

'I asked my moms if we could have it tonight, so I hope so.'

Liam sneezed loudly again.

'Get that boy a tissue and take the books to your classroom. I don't want him making a mess.' Yeats turned his back on them as if to say the conversation was over.

'*Oh, I was also wondering about those junk monsters. How to get rid of them, how they are made...*' Nora began.

'*No sashimi, no extra requests. Figure out the Dewey Decimal System. It's not hard. Turns out, not everything is on a computer.*' Yeats stuck his tail straight up in the air and leapt from one table to another and then to a bookshelf before trotting away.

"*I don't think he likes me,*" Liam said sniffily.

"*You should probably figure out a way to change that. He seems to know a lot around here. I wonder if we could ask him about what happened last year.*" Nora thought out loud as they made their way over to the ladder leading up to the second story of book shelves.

"How do you know he's telling you the truth? He's not only a cat, but also a faerie creature. We don't know anything about him," Liam said while wiping his nose on his sleeve.

"You're right, and we're in a library. We should look up what information there is on Cat Siths along with Pukwudgies and Junk Monsters," Nora said. "Check for the Pukwudgie books where Yeats said they'd be. I'll go figure out the card catalogue and hopefully find the books we're looking for."

"I'm going to need some allergy meds if this is going to become a thing." Liam sighed dramatically and started climbing the stairs up to the second story. There was a ledge with a railing that encompassed the room for people to stand on once they got to the second story. However, if the books were too far up, they would have to climb another ladder, which may have been sturdy but certainly didn't appear to be.

Nora hurried to the card catalogues and found that it was much easier to navigate than she had thought. Eventually she had written down the letters and numbers of the books they were trying to find. Everything was arranged alphabetically by subject. All of the books of a type of lore were together, such as faerie folklore by country, Japanese Yokai, Native American Spirits, etc. After nervously watching Liam hang from the ladders while holding books, she sent him after several more. He seemed to sneeze less when the result could mean plummeting ten or more feet to the ground.

Sifting through the books, Nora selected the three she thought were the most helpful and left the others in the Return Bin. She wondered if Yeats was the one putting them away or if there was some sort of magic that would do it for him. How did he pick up large books with his cute little paws and mouth?

Bringing their books to the glass classroom, they began to sort through them. Liam was most interested in the Pukwudgies, after finding all of those quills. He skimmed through the pages and showed Nora some of the pictures. "It says here that they live in the woods and stay away from buildings and populated areas. They are protective of their forests and are known to play mean tricks on people, kidnap them, and even poison or kill people! Why would Mrs. M let kids go outside with those things nearby? They could get mad and hurt somebody!"

Nora shared his concern. "She said they had an agreement though. Maybe they're not as bad as they seem. Also, why would the quills from one of them bring us up to the building? Something isn't right about all this. I don't think I want to see one in person anymore."

"They could be trying to kidnap someone or do something mean! We should tell Mrs. M or Mr. Walker. It might already be too late." Liam got up from the desk and marched out of the room.

Nora had no choice but to follow him. She wasn't sure if they were over-reacting, but she agreed with Liam. If the Pukwudgies were mad at someone and they were as dangerous as the book said, they needed to warn people. Approaching Mr. Walker's office, the door was closed. There were hushed voices coming from behind the door.

Liam knocked loudly. The voices stopped and Mrs. M opened the door. Inside the room, Mr. Walker was sitting at his desk. Maria and Kimi were both sitting in chairs nearby. Mrs. M squinted at them from behind her dark-framed glasses.

"Yes? Did you need something?"

"Uh, yeah," Liam wasn't expecting to have such an audience. "We were reading about the Pukwudgies and we saw quills leading up to the side of the school, so we wanted to..."

Mrs. M cut him off. "Didn't I tell you to leave the Pukwudgies alone?"

Nora stepped in. "Yes, but we are worried they might be doing something to someone at school."

"Don't be ridiculous. The Pukwudgies stay away from buildings and people. They don't like us and avoid us at all costs. You should do the same with them." Mrs. M said. "If that is all, I'm afraid we are in the middle of something."

Kimi smiled at them apologetically, but Maria refused to make eye contact. Mr. Walker was about to stand up when Mrs. M. closed the door.

"She didn't even listen to us!" Liam practically yelled when they returned to the glass classroom.

Nora was glad for the sound-proof walls.

"I know." Nora agreed. "Something's going on and they don't want us to know about it."

"Fine, we don't need their help. We'll figure out what the Pukwudgies are up to on our own." Liam slammed his notebook on the desk and began angrily drawing a picture similar to the Pukwudgie in the book. His hand flew across the page as he made the quills longer than they needed to be.

"Ok, why don't you take notes on the Pukwudgies and I'll look into the junk monster." Nora skimmed through several passages on animating garbage and clutter. Each reference in the book noted that a powerful, magical creature created the monster in order to protect or hide something. There was no instance of a junk monster spontaneously creating itself. However, sometimes the creatures seemed to take a life of their own and grow larger feeding on misplaced objects and the anxiety a person had from losing the objects. "I think something would have had to create the junk monster in the first place and then either whatever creates it gets rid of it or the thing gets too big for the magic that created it. I actually don't see any example of a junk monster hurting anyone who didn't try to take a piece of it. Mostly people see it moving and run away." Nora shrugged.

Liam put his pen down. He seemed to have calmed a bit. "Ok, sounds like that will sort itself out, except why did someone make that thing?" Liam squinted at his own reflection in the glass wall.

"I don't know. I suppose I'm not even sure it's a junk monster, Yeats told me not to focus too much on one possibility." Nora recalled.

"Yeats? What does that book say about Cat Siths?" Liam pointed to the thick, well-used book on faerie folklore.

Nora turned to the index and then found the section about Cat Siths. "They are Irish faeries. Some people believe they are a bad omen and can steal souls while others think they are highly intelligent and bless the houses of those who are friendly to them." Nora shrugged. "Not really a lot here.

It says to be very careful making deals with them and they can change their size, some can get as big as a house."

"None of that sounds like we should trust him at all." Liam began to write those words on the page with his drawing of Yeats.

"It doesn't say that. Yeats has been nothing but helpful. He just acts like a cat. I think you're letting your runny nose get in the way of getting to know him." Nora said.

"And I think you're letting your love of cats get in the way of seeing what he really is." Liam would shift his attention from his paper while he spoke.

Nora huffed. "He's kind of a cat. And if you understand cats, it's easier to understand him. Without the teachers or older students being open with us or helping us with the Pukwudgies, I think we're going to need Yeats if we want to find out how to deal with them."

Liam sighed. "You're probably right. I'll get some allergy meds."

They did not have much time left in the school day. There was no sign of Yeats when they returned their books to the library. In fact, there was no sign of anyone in the Secret Wing. No students or teachers. Nora suggested that they look for Mrs. M to make sure it was OK to go back to regular classes, so they went to the hallway with the large fish tank. They watched the jellyfish float around, calmly for a few minutes before Liam grew restless.

"We should just head back. My mom might get here early to pick me up, and I want to make sure she knows to drop me off at your place so we can do homework together." Liam said.

"Wyrd homework or homework, homework?" Nora asked.

"Actual homework. I've been working on my notebook in class, so I have no idea what we're supposed to be doing."

Nora was about to respond, when a dark, inky creature suddenly flew through the water like a bolt of black lightning. It smashed into one of the jellyfish, completely enveloping it. In an instant, the jellyfish was gone, and the goopy, almost translucent creature was staring at them through the glass with the large eyes of a baby animal.

"Wow, that is terrifying and also, kinda cute," Liam said.

"I was thinking the same thing." Nora put her fingers up to the glass.

The dark, purple creature rubbed its head against the glass as if it were trying to nuzzle her fingertips. When its head hit the glass it squished flat revealing its lack of bones and then popped back into a round shape when it backed away.

"I take it back. It's not kinda cute, it's adorable."

They took turns pretending to pet it through the glass, and it responded with sweet faces and rubbing its head next to them, its body changing shape but returning to a sort of round head with gooey appendages, like a tennis ball wrapped in a handkerchief. Occasionally it did a few flips to show off. After a few minutes, it went back into the rocks it had been hiding in.

"We should go," Nora said as soon as the creature was out of sight.

Liam agreed, so they quit searching for any teachers and went back to their regular classrooms to finish up the rest of the day.

Nora's seat partner was absent for the ride home, so it was easier for her to sense to AJ without having to make awkward small-talk. *'Liam told me that there might be something going on with the buses.'*

AJ didn't have to try to act normal. Everyone already assumed he was strange, so he simply leaned forward on the seat so he could see Nora better. The student next to him stared out the window pretending not to notice.

'Yes, we need to look around for anything out of the ordinary. That rubbery stuff on the outside of the seats is a cover that zips on. You can actually unzip it and feel around the inside of the seat foam.' AJ unzipped the bottom of one in front of him, which happened to be the back of Nora's to demonstrate.

As he ran his hand over the foam, Nora could feel him behind her. She didn't think she could do the same without getting the attention of the kids in front of her, but she had to check it out. She unzipped the bottom and ran her hands along the foam. It was old and crumbled under her touch. Pulling out her hand, she soon found her fingers covered in pieces of foam. "Yuck." She said.

"What are you doing?" One of the boys in front of her asked.

She tried to think of what Liam would say in this situation. "Uh, I didn't realize these things could unzip. Pretty cool."

When she pointed it out, other students began to fiddle with the zippers on the seats. Some felt the foam underneath, while others purposely jabbed the kids in front of them.

'Good work,' AJ sent, *'if there is something out of the ordinary, one of them might find it.'*

But while AJ and Nora watched the students playing with their seats, Skip bellowed. "You kids better not be messing with my seats! Zip those back up, and get your hands out of there! What do you think this is, your mom's couch? You ruin one seat, and I'll be sending the bill to your parents!" It seemed like an angry but appropriate response at first. Then he continued. "You good-for-nothing children think you can just get away with anything. Well, I'm here to tell you, you can't. Not one of you will amount to anything. All you do is use up everything we give you. You're all roaches, good for nothing roaches!"

The bus went quiet. Some of the kids seemed annoyed, others nervous. They had never heard an adult go on such a tirade before. Hatred was oozing from every word. AJ watched Skip intently for the rest of the bus ride. Nora, however, took the time to search over her seat, check the windows and the floor visually. There was nothing unusual. A few kids in the seat across were playing with the purple slime and whispering to each other.

When the bus approached her stop, she subtly nodded to AJ and took her time walking to the front so she could look over the other students' seats. Before she got to the steps, she fumbled with her backpack so she could visually inspect the driver's seat.

"We haven't got all day," Skip growled.

In response, Nora rushed down the steps and out the door. Liam was already waiting at her bus stop. Mrs. Kelly must have dropped him off there. When they got into Nora's house, they tried to focus on their science or math homework, but they kept going back to the supernatural. Their minds were aflutter with questions. Why was there a Pukwudgie going up to the school? How could they protect themselves if Pukwudgies were as dangerous as they were made out to be? What was going on with the bus? How would they get a ride to the marshes to investigate the bus yard? What were the teachers and the older students in the Secret Wing hiding from them?

After a very distracted homework session (especially after Nora's sister got home), they eventually got their work mostly done. Nora decided to walk Liam home so they could talk about properly labeling and storing his notebooks.

"What if we put them under my bed?" Liam suggested, while zipping up his coat against the chilly breeze.

"I kind of liked what you said about hiding in plain sight. Maybe we should just put them on a shelf with other notebooks?" Nora said as they approached Liam's house.

"That's actually brilliant. Too obvious." Stopping in his tracks, Liam moaned. "Uck, my dad's here. That means my parents are probably going to fight over dinner."

Nora patted his shoulder apologetically. "You wanna eat at my house? Momma T agreed to pick up some sushi and sashimi for me. They were really surprised when I asked for it but then decided we should *expand our palates and refine our tastes* or something like that."

"Yuck, no thanks. I guess that horrible cat will be happy," Liam said morosely, "I better get in there before one of them starts throwing stuff."

Waving goodbye, Nora headed back to her house. She had never actually had sushi before and hoped she would like it. Though, she was positive Emaline would probably throw a fit, since she hated fish. It was worth it if she could get some information out of Yeats, maybe even find out what everyone was hiding.

CHAPTER 11

Streaks of sunlight rained through the glass dome of the library, giving the room a distinctive zebra-like appearance. Mrs. M had been busy again on errands which left Liam and Nora to their own devices. They preferred it that way anyway. Liam had taken his allergy medication, which made him a little more drowsy than usual. The two of them had taken to sitting on the plush carpet of the library, surrounding themselves with books instead of using the tables.

Yeats was nowhere to be seen for most of the morning, which didn't surprise Nora, because cats generally had long sleeping schedules during the mid-morning. When he finally approached the two of them, they were sitting in a pile of over a dozen books.

'*Make yourselves at home,*' Yeats sensed, grumpily. His fur did not appear as sleekly smoothed back as it usually did and his eyes were only half open.

'*Morning Yeats,*' Nora sensed with a smile on her face. '*Why do you think a Pukwudgie would come up to the building?*'

'*It wouldn't,*' Yeats replied before resting his head on Nora's lap for pets.

'*We followed its quills up to the side of the school,*' Liam sensed to Yeats.

Yeats acted as if Liam wasn't there, by turning his back to him and addressing Nora as he spoke. '*Quills? Loose quills, you say? That's odd, how many?*'

'*At least ten, maybe more,*' Nora replied.

Yeat's head popped up now, as though his interest had peaked. '*That's too many. Any blood?*'

'*No, just quills.*' Liam answered.

'*How very strange.*' Yeats stared off into the distance, the pupils of his large eyes shrinking to thin slits against the light. '*Pukwudgies don't shed, or molt. They only tend to lose a few quills here and there in a fight. Which means, something is very wrong with one of the Pukwudgies behind the school.*'

'*What do you think would cause that?*' Nora asked.

'*I'm not sure. There's a book in here somewhere with ailments or curses of magical creatures, not to be confused with the many books about ailments or curses from magical creatures.*' Yeats said.

'*Great, where is it?*' Nora asked.

'*Well, No-Rah, I would be willing to go find it for you for the sashimi I can smell in your backpack.*' Yeats licked his lips. The dark pupils had expanded to fill his large eyes.

Nora was hoping to use the tuna to draw out more information from Yeats but did not expect him to be able to smell it through her bag and lunchbox. '*Oh fine. I was going to give it to you anyway.*' She pulled six pieces of fish out, three tuna and three salmon. They were sliced and placed on a plastic tray.

As soon as Nora opened the lid, Yeats bounded onto her lap. He opened his mouth much larger than a cat his size should have been able to and swallowed down the entire contents of the tray in one gulp. He then licked his paw daintily.

Liam's eyes were wide when he looked to Nora. She met his gaze with a similar surprised expression.

'*Delicious*,' he sensed before flicking his tail and leaping onto a high shelf. He sped off to the back of the library where they could no longer see him.

"I keep forgetting he's not really a cat," Nora said.

Before Liam could respond, the door to the library pushed open. A boy peeked his head around the corner. He had dark, slicked back hair and tan skin. After stepping into the room, he closed the door. Once he noticed Liam and Nora sitting on the floor, he smiled and waved while approaching them. Nora soon recognized the boy as the one who was selling slime in the lunchroom.

"S'up," he walked over to them and took a seat beside them. He wasn't carrying the backpack with slime that Nora saw him with before. "So you're the new Wyrd students? I'm Carlos, nice to meet you. How do you like it here? That cat around?" He inspected the library trying to see if there was anything hidden in the shelves.

"Thought your name was 'Fresh?'" Nora said. Something about this kid was making her uncomfortable. She wasn't sure if it was his too-wide smile or the vacant look in his eyes.

"That's the guy who tried to sell you slime?" Liam asked.

Carlos laughed. "Yeah, yeah, that's just a nickname I came up with. What are you two working on here?" He picked up one of the open books and eyed the pages.

"I don't think you can make up your own nickname," Liam said.

"Who are you, the nickname police?" Carlos said.

Just then, there was a loud cat yowl and Yeats flew at the book Carlos was holding, knocking it to the floor. 'Get Back!' Yeats sensed. His eyes were glowing green as he hissed and brandished his claws.

"Not the friendliest of welcomes," Carlos said.

'*Put your rings on, children, and run straight to Mr. Walker's room. Do not look back!*' Yeats, somehow, sensed to them loudly as if he were yelling.

Not knowing what else to do, Liam and Nora did just as Yeats had instructed. Nora slipped her ring back onto her thumb and followed Liam to hop over their mess of books. They rushed past Carlos, who crossed his arms over his chest and watched them leave with a smirk. They ran as fast as they could straight to Mr. Walker's office at the end of the hall. When they got to the room, his door was open. They were breathing heavily, more from the excitement than the short run.

Mr. Walker was sitting at his desk studying some papers. Little metal balls clacked against one another on the rack on top of his desk. Visibly startled, Mr. Walker jumped to his feet. He was wearing a teal button down, stretched tightly over his immense stomach.

"What's wrong? Are you alright?" He asked, his face instantly red.

'*There's a boy in the library, Carlos?*' Nora sensed, because it was easier than talking at the moment. '*Yeats told us to come straight here. What's going on?*'

"Oh dear, this is no good, no good at all." He pulled a silver bell, the size of his fist out of his desk. "Stay in this room. Lock the door, with *all* the locks, behind me once I leave. Do not open the door for anyone, including me, unless you hear these words in this exact order: Unicorn, Tangerine, Sofa." Mr. Walker left without waiting for a confirmation from Liam or Nora. He closed the door behind him, leaving the two of them staring at it.

Liam began to work the complicated locking mechanisms on the door. There was a simple slide lock, one with a chain, a strange twisting gear, and several levers. Nora assisted. The two of them sat in chairs opposite each other once they were done. Taking everything in, Nora eyed the motivational posters hung on the walls containing a kitten or puppy with a pun printed in bubble letters. It was a small room with a desk, a lamp, a filing cabinet and flat-topped wooden chest.

"What just happened?" Nora asked.

"I have no idea, but we better get some answers. If that Carlos kid is as dangerous as everyone was acting, we need to know what we're facing." Liam searched around Mr. Walker's desk for a pen and paper. He had left his notebook in the library.

Opening the top drawer, Liam stopped before reaching his hand in. The drawer was almost bursting with random objects, straws, pocket-watches, tape, rubber band balls, and pens. He took out one pen and clicked it repeatedly.

"I thought he looked too old to be here when he was selling slime in the lunchroom" Nora said. She pushed a legal-size notepad over to Liam.

After clicking the pen a final time, and deciding it wasn't going to do anything out of the ordinary, he accepted the legal pad to take notes.

"*Fresh?* What a terrible nickname. Who would call themselves that?" Liam wrote "Fresh" across the top and added stink lines as well as poop emojis.

"He must be some sort of supernatural creature. He's not a student." Nora theorized. "It's hard to tell if Yeats recognized him or just knew he wasn't supposed to be there."

Liam nodded while writing down bullet points. "Yeats told us to put the rings on. Mr. Walker said the iron protects against faeries and some demonic presences, and the silver should protect against certain spirits, werewolves maybe? It doesn't really narrow it down much."

"We're definitely at a disadvantage. He knows who and what we are, but we know nothing about him, except that he doesn't belong here."

"And that we should be afraid of him," Liam added. "We have to assume he's dangerous and powerful."

"Do you think this has something to do with the secret they're keeping about the older kids?" Nora asked.

"I have a feeling it does," Liam agreed, and then squinted up at the old-fashioned clock on the wall. "We're going to be late for regular class. And I actually did the homework this time!"

Nora smiled. Regular class was the least of her worries right now. There was some supernatural creature who knew how to get into the Secret Wing and recognized them. He could be anywhere in the school and Nora had no idea what he wanted.

Just then there was a knock on the door.

"Uh...Unicorn...Tangerine...Something-er-other" said a voice that sounded like Cam.

"Sofa," AJ's voice corrected him.

Liam and Nora went through the long process of opening the door to find Cam and AJ waiting outside. AJ had recently fixed his glasses with masking tape, which suited his overall style with the hiked up pants and a baggy jacket. Cam, on the other hand, was wearing a basketball jersey and pristine sneakers.

They walked in and went through the process of relocking the door. AJ took Mr. Walker's seat behind his desk and Cam sat on top of the desk, since there were no more chairs. The office was beginning to feel a little cramped with four students in it.

"Do you two know what's going on?" Liam asked them.

They both shook their heads earnestly.

Cam explained. "We came in for our classes and Mr. Walker just told us to come straight here, say those words and lock the door."

"We were in the library when this Carlos kid came in and then Yeats had us put our rings on and run here." Nora said.

AJ and Cam exchanged looks.

"Who is Carlos? What is Carlos?" Nora was slightly annoyed that she had to ask.

"The only Carlos we know is Maria's older brother," AJ replied.

"Maria's brother?" Liam asked. "But this kid had to be something supernatural."

"Then maybe it's just taking the shape of Maria's brother," AJ offered.

Cam nodded. "Yeah, he moved in with his grandparents in Puerto Rico after everything happened last year."

"What happened last year?!" Liam was getting as annoyed as Nora.

"We don't really know," Cam said with a sigh. "They kept us away from all of it. Something kept happening with all the older kids. Accidents and bad things until Mrs. M and Mr. Walker gathered all the older kids together saying they'd put an end to it."

"We were left in the dark about most of it. They had other tasks for us to do to keep us away from what was going on. But I know it has to do with the fae, because they were all prepared with iron that day." AJ said.

"After whatever happened, most of the kids were still upset and decided to go to other schools. The only ones who stayed were Maria and Kimi." Cam said. He brushed his red braids out of his face and tied them back behind his ears.

"Aren't you mad that they didn't tell you?" Nora asked, "I'd be constantly trying to figure out what happened."

"We are, and we have. But, the teachers are in charge. They can make sure we don't find certain things or only find the bits of information they want us to," AJ said, "I think they are just trying to protect us."

"Or cover up a mistake," Liam said.

"Maybe," AJ replied, "but I've only ever known Mrs. M and Mr. Walker to want to help us. They seem to believe in us and have honestly been the best teachers I've ever had."

Nora could tell they were making AJ uncomfortable. He kept scratching the back of his head and adjusting his glasses as they spoke.

"Me too," Cam admitted. "They actually listen to us and help us do what *we* want to do, not just what they think we should...normally."

"So that's it, you're just going to let them cover up whatever happened? You're not even going to try to figure out what's going on with Carlos?" Nora could not contain herself. Before she knew it, she was standing and yelling with her fists balled up. It was unlike her, but this was more than she could take.

There was silence for a moment before AJ spoke.

"No. I trust Mrs. M and Mr. Walker to be doing what they think is best for us, but if they won't tell us the truth about what happened, then we're going to find out for ourselves."

"Are you sure about this?" Cam asked. "We tried last year and hit a lot of dead ends before Mrs. M cut back our library hours."

"I don't care." AJ turned to meet Liam and then Nora's eyes. "We're with you on this."

Suddenly there was a loud knock on the door and Mr. Walker's voice saying, "Unicorn, Tangerine, Sofa."

Liam ripped the paper he had been taking notes on out of the legal pad and folded it before sliding it into his pocket. He then dropped the pen back into the drawer. After unlocking all of the doors, they admitted a smiling Mr. Walker into the room.

"Nothing more to worry about, kids," he said, though he was wringing his hands together nervously. "We won't be having any more issues with that particular problem. I'll be writing late passes for Nora and Liam. AJ and Cam can head to the classroom, where Mrs. M has a lesson for you. Let us enjoy the rest of our day." Mr. Walker placed the passes on his desk and then searched around for a pen. Opening the drawer with the pen Liam had used in it, he peered down as if contemplating and then shook his head. He then found one in his pocket and jotted down the information on the passes.

"Is Yeats OK?" Nora had to ask. Even though she knew Yeats was a powerful faerie creature, she had no idea what Carlos was.

"Hmm?" Mr. Walker was distracted, "Yeats? Of course, he's just fine. You can visit with him tomorrow if you like, but you must be on your way. You're already late for class."

They filed out of Mr. Walker's room. AJ and Liam walked ahead, talking about the school bus. Cam lingered behind a bit and got Nora's attention.

"Hey, Nora?" he asked while shoving his hands in the pockets of his track pants.

She stopped next to Cam, remembering what she had found out about the junk monster and thinking about how to tell him about it quickly.

"I just wanted to say, I'm really sorry about yesterday," he said.

"Yesterday?"

"Uh, yeah. That thing I said. I said you had a crush on me. That was really embarrassing and I just couldn't think of anything on the spot like that." He went on before Nora could respond. "So, next time, if something like that happens, I'll say I have a crush on you. It's only fair, right?"

Nora felt flushed again. "No, I mean, I appreciate the gesture, but it's OK. We can think up an excuse or just make sure we aren't seen together again."

"Oh," Cam said, looking a little disappointed. "Does this mean you don't want to figure out what's going on with all the missing stuff with me?"

"No!" Nora said, realizing they had fallen a little too far behind and quickened her pace to catch up with Liam, "I found out more about junk monsters. I was going to tell you about it. I think we should definitely keep trying to figure out if that's what it is."

"OK, cool," Cam said before turning the direction of the glass classroom, and then added. "Glad we're cool."

Liam was waiting for Nora by the entrance to the Secret Wing glancing back. "Our backpacks and all of our stuff is still in the library."

"Crap," Nora said. "Should we go back and get it?"

"I didn't do all that homework just to go to class empty handed. Also, our lunches are in there." He pointed out.

As they were about to turn back, Kimi almost ran into them. Her multiple bracelets slid up her arms when she held up their backpacks. "Looking for these?"

"Thanks," Liam said, taking his blue bag and opening it to examine the contents.

"I'm pretty sure we got everything, and it was easy to figure out what belonged in which bag." Kimi added to Liam. "That notebook of yours is pretty cool."

"You looked at it?!" his pale cheeks flushed.

"Not really, just flipped through the pictures. If you draw me, do it anime style." Kimi smiled.

Realizing Kimi was the exact person Nora wanted to talk to about what had happened with the older kids and that the hallways were empty, Nora decided now was as good a time as any. 'Did you know Carlos?'

'Carlos?' Kimi was taken back. '*Uh, yeah, Maria's brother. We were all friends with him. But, I didn't spend much time with him.*'

'*Did he really move to Puerto Rico?*' Liam asked.

It seemed like a sensible question to rule out that the boy they had met was not the real Carlos.

'*Yeah, he had a rough time last year and his parents thought he was acting out too much, so they sent him to help out his grandparents, learn his roots or something.'* Kimi leaned against a locker in the hallway. *'Why are you asking about him?'*

'Did you get along with him?' Nora continued before answering.

'Uh, sure. He and I found Inky, that cute gooky thing in the fish tank with the jellyfish, together. It was kind of a funny story, I actually almost stepped on it...seriously though, why are you asking?' The smile on Kimi's face had faded.

'There was a boy in the library calling himself, 'Carlos,' and Yeats and Mr. Walker got really upset about it.' Liam replied.

'What? Well, it couldn't have been him... I have to go and you two need to get to class.' Kimi turned around briskly and made no effort to hide how quickly she needed to get into the Secret Wing.

'I don't really feel like that got us any answers.' Nora sighed and slipped her backpack over her shoulders.

'I just have more questions,' Liam agreed, *'We can talk about this at lunch and recess. Remember our secret code word in case there's trouble?'*

'Of course.' Nora sensed. When they first started seeing supernatural oddities, Liam had come up with a codeword for either of them to say when they needed to take a situation seriously. They only used it in very rare situations when they needed to get the other's attention quickly.

'Good.' He picked up his pace toward his class and Nora did the same.

It was hard to focus in her class before lunch. There were so many questions buzzing through her mind that she wondered how any Wyrd student was able to live a double life. Obviously AJ's status in the eyes of his peers was suffering, but the rest seemed to be doing all right as far as Nora could tell. She had never been the best at keeping secrets either. After accidentally telling her sister about a big surprise party at the zoo that her moms were planning, they decided no more surprise parties. If it weren't for Liam, Nora feared she would have let a secret slip to one of her classmates by now.

CHAPTER 12

'*I wonder if there's a way to find out who the previous Wyrd students were?*' Liam sensed while chomping down on his bologna sandwich.

'*I can't believe anyone eats that stuff. Maybe, but it's not like they just have a list of students lying around. I have art class with Maria again tomorrow, but I doubt she'll tell me anything.*' Nora peeled the clementine she had brought and offered Liam a slice.

'*AJ eats bologna sandwiches.*' Liam stuck his tongue out. '*He said you two didn't find anything on the school bus, but you may have gotten Skip's attention. I don't think you should do anything else that might get you in trouble. There's a comic book and game store about a mile and a half from the marshes, in that plaza with the old people clothes. I think we can get my dad to drop us off there for a while, and then we'll have to walk.*' Liam accepted the slice and shoved it into his mouth without even swallowing the piece of sandwich that was in there.

Nora wrinkled her nose. '*OK, when do you want to go?*'

'*I'll see if AJ can come this weekend. Can you ask Cam when you see him next?*'

'*Sure, but I'll probably see AJ on the bus before you see him, and you might see Cam before me.*' Nora pointed out.

'*I guess, just seems like you and Cam have been hanging out a lot lately.*' Liam continued to stare at his food even though Nora was trying to make eye contact.

'*Not really,*' Nora finally sensed back when Liam wouldn't meet her eyes. '*And you're helping with the junk monster now too, so you can help us search places.*'

Visibly relaxing his shoulders, Liam finished the rest of his lunch. They waited anxiously for the bell to ring so they could explore outside once again. As soon as it did, they rushed out to seek more quills. They were not difficult to find. This time, there seemed to be a quill every few feet or so. Following the trail around the building, it led deeper into the woods. The air was getting chillier each day, and the orange pine-needles on the ground were browning and snapping under their feet.

"I don't know if we should follow it into the woods," Nora said, peering back to see if the teacher had spotted them off of the wooden pathways.

"Probably not," Liam agreed then stopped. "Hey, what's that?"

There was an object glittering beneath the pine needles. Even though it was mostly covered, it was reflecting the light. Liam brushed the needles aside to reveal a gold necklace with letters engraved on it. "Fancy," he said.

When they held it up to examine it, the voice of another student could be heard from the boarded path beside them. "Hey, Ava, does that freak have your necklace?"

Ava and another girl rushed down the boarded path, their boots sounding like hooved animals. Once Ava got closer to them, she squinted in their direction, stepped off of the path and crunched onto the needles. The other girls noisily followed after her. Ava passed a handful of slime to one of the other girls before marching up to Liam and ripping the necklace out of his hand.

"That is *my* necklace. I put it in my backpack this morning, so this little creep must have gone into my locker!" Ava shouted before shoving Liam, hard in the chest.

"Hey!" Nora yelled while Liam stumbled a few steps backward. "He didn't go in your locker, we were in the East Wing all morning!"

"I don't care if you two were making out in the sped closet. You took my necklace, and when I tell the teacher, you'll be suspended." Ava's nose was turned slightly upward in the air as she spoke. She tucked her necklace into her pink fleece vest.

Her two friends giggled meanly.

"We just found it out here on the ground!" Liam insisted. "Maybe you dropped it."

"I didn't drop it! You stole it!" She began yelling. "Teacher, teacher!"

Nora recognized her art teacher's flurry of curls as she made her way to them. She was wearing a long, dark coat with splashes of paint on the sleeves. "What are you kids doing off the paths? You know the rules." She said, but even her reprimanding voice sounded friendly and airy.

"They stole my necklace! Take them to the office!" Ava ordered pointing at Liam and Nora.

"We just found it. We saw it on the side of the path and came down to pick it up," Nora explained.

"They're lying!" Ava said while motioning to the other two girls to back her up.

"You two go back to the school," the art teacher said to the girls when she saw them. "Young lady, I think you need to calm down."

"Calm down! Are you crazy?! This is a real, gold necklace! Just because you can't afford one on a teacher salary..."

"That is quite enough, young lady. You do not speak to teachers that way!" She cut Ava off. It was obvious that the art teacher almost never lost her cool, but what Ava said must have been too much. "You are going to apologize to these two and thank them for finding your necklace or you will be spending every afternoon each week cleaning the clay out of the kiln in the art room."

"But..." Ava began, then saw the anger rising in the art teacher's face. "Fine!" With her head down, she grumbled. "Thank you for finding my necklace. Sorry for what I said."

"Good, now you will be coming with me so we can further discuss how to be respectful," the art teacher turned without looking to make sure anyone followed.

The other teachers began blowing their whistles and waving for students to go back to the building. Ava stomped back to the path after the art teacher. As they began to climb back onto the pathway, Nora almost fell back. There was something hiding under the walkway, a few feet from them. All she could see was a dark, lopsided mass, but it was definitely moving. Her breath caught in her throat, but Liam offered Nora a hand up. Once she joined Liam, she quickened her pace to the school.

"What's the rush?" Liam asked nonchalantly.

"There's something under the path," Nora said in a hushed voice, "Don't look back." They walked hastily down the pathway back to school. When they were farther away Liam said. "What was it?"

"I don't know. I couldn't get a good look," Nora said.

"It could be the junk monster. Maybe that's why the necklace was there," Liam pointed out just as they reached the end of the walkway and stepped down onto the bit of grass before the building.

'*Or maybe a Pukwudgie,*' Nora sensed to Liam once they joined their classmates to go into the building.

'*So, are we going to talk about how awful Ava was being? Like, I've seen her be nasty to other kids, but she's always been a suck-up to the teachers.*' Liam opened the door for Nora and they went over to his locker.

'*Do you think the junk monster makes people...I don't know, angrier if it's around?*' Nora wondered, but she hadn't seen anything about it in her books, and neither she nor Liam seemed any different. Maybe Ava was just really upset about her necklace. Either way, she certainly wasn't going to be happy with Liam or Nora any time soon. Nora worried she would retaliate in some way.

'*Is there anything we can do to clear things up with those girls?*' she sensed to Liam, but it was almost more to herself.

Sucking in a breath, Liam shook his head. '*You need to stop worrying about what everyone else thinks about you. Not everyone's going to like us, no matter what we do.*'

'*I know that. I just wish we didn't draw so much attention.*'

'*Well, you can't be extraordinary and fly under the radar forever. Why do you get all A's if you don't want people to notice?*'

Nora had never thought about it like that before. She was always trying so hard to succeed at everything, but secretly hoped no one would pick up on it. Why did attention make her so uncomfortable? Did she think people wouldn't like her if she did well in school or even tried to? No matter how much she denied it, she really did want people to like her. If she could only be like Liam who seemed to carelessly do whatever he wanted, things would be so much easier.

The sound of Liam slamming his locker closed yanked Nora out of her head.

He smiled at her the same way he always did when she was lost in thought. '*We have a lot to think about, but I have to go to this stupid family counseling thing with my parents tonight. I'll take notes, and we can catch up tomorrow.*' Liam sensed while holding up his notebook. '*If you hear or see that Carlos guy, promise me you won't go near him. Everyone seems so worried about him, he's got to be dangerous.*'

'*Same goes for you. If we're going to get information on him, we'll do it together.*' Nora and Liam fist-bumped and went their separate ways to their classes.

Nora had PE and for the first time she had to change into gym clothes. After spending some time in the familiar locker room changing into her shorts and t-shirt along with a few other girls that she had been friendly with, like Mia from science class, she noticed that Penelope was changing in the corner and avoiding anyone's gaze. The locker room was very different with students in it. It still smelled musty, but the buzz of the heater was less obvious through the voices of students and with all of the belongings strewn around the room it no longer felt abandoned. Even the flickering overhead light was far less ominous with other students laughing and talking about their day.

When Nora realized Penelope was still keeping to herself, she motioned to Mia and the two of them walked over. Penelope was tightening her shoe laces while they approached. She winced when they drew close.

"I heard we're playing volleyball today," Mia started, "maybe we can pick our own teams."

"We should try to be on a team together," Nora suggested.

Penelope relaxed immediately. "That would be cool."

As the three of them headed to the door, Penelope caught the back of Nora's shirt. Nora turned to see Penelope wringing her hands.

"I'm sorry about before, in homeroom," she said in a voice so quiet it was almost a whisper.

Nora smiled back. "It's OK."

"And, I'm sorry about the rumors we were spreading about you and Liam. I know you're just friends." She continued a little bit louder.

Even though Nora felt a twinge of anger along with her curiosity about the rumors, she managed to keep a smile on her face and shrug.

Penelope went on as if she was bursting with more to say. "I also really like your rainbow barrettes. I think they're cool. I wish I had them," Penelope fumbled with her bangs as if to show how useful a barrette would be.

Almost on instinct, Nora reached into her bag and took out the rainbow barrettes. After passing one to Penelope, who immediately pulled back her bangs with it, she affixed the other to her own hair. The two of them grinned at one another in the mirror before leaving the locker room together. Once they were in the gym, she realized that there were sixth graders in the room as well, including Cam. When the teacher went through the attendance, Cam glanced over to Nora.

"We will be dividing into groups of four, three fifth graders and one sixth grader. The sixth grader will be showing the fifth graders the different ways to hit a volleyball, and you will have a chance to practice with a net. We won't get to an actual game today, just practice hitting back and forth over the nets that are set up. Fifth-graders get into groups of three and sixth-graders, find a group." The teacher then blew his whistle as if that was how he ended all conversations.

Nora was glad she already had a group, and so were her two companions. Cam had made a beeline for them as soon as the whistle was blown. He introduced himself to all of them, including Nora as if they didn't know one another. He then got a volleyball and proceeded to show them the different ways to hit it.

'Hey, can you start with Mia? I want to talk to Penelope for a little bit.' Nora sensed to Cam.

He made no indication that he heard her, but then took Mia over to the nets to practice. The two of them volleyed back and forth better than Nora expected them to.

Sitting in the bleachers as they waited for their turn, Nora turned to Penelope. "Those girls in homeroom are pretty mean, but I didn't think you'd hit that girl... Jess?"

Penelope sighed. "Everyone keeps asking me what happened, but it's all just a blur. I remember being so mad, and then everything went red. It's so embarrassing."

Nora had to find out if there was a link to the junk monster but wasn't sure where to begin. "The fight started because one of you lost something?"

Shaking her head, Penelope went on. "No, we were playing with that slime stuff, and I think Jess took mine. I don't really know. I blanked out. My parents are telling everyone that those girls were bullying me, so I have in-school suspension next week instead of out of school."

"Were they? Bullying you?"

"I don't know. They were mean, and I was scared of them. The vice principal said we're both lucky we aren't being expelled. Jess has to do community service." Penelope covered her face in her hands and repeated, "It's all just so embarrassing."

Nora couldn't think of anything to say to make her feel better. She suspected something supernatural was causing the girls to act out, but there was no way she could tell Penelope that without sounding like a crazy person. So she just said, "Everyone will forget about it soon, and it's good to stand up for yourself sometimes."

"I hope so. People keep looking at me like I'm going to fly off the handle at any minute. I'm really not like that," as she said this, Mia was heading back their way and Cam was motioning for one of them to come over.

Getting up to join Cam, Nora said, "I know."

Cam passed Nora the volleyball and made arm motions to show her how to set it and spike it but wasn't talking. He sensed to her, *'What's going on?'*

'That girl up there, Penelope, is really quiet and nice. Yesterday she attacked a sixth-grader, Jess, in homeroom for taking her slime. It's really not like her.' Nora sensed to Cam while hitting the ball up and down poorly.

'And then today, a girl who normally sucks up to teachers told one of the teachers off. She was really mad about this necklace we found of hers outside.'

'Jess can be kinda mean, but it sounds like everyone's acting all aggro. You think this has to do with the buses? The drivers are like that too.' Cam suggested.

'I didn't even think about that. Maybe.' Nora pondered for a minute, 'I thought maybe it had to do with the junk monster, because we found the necklace right before that happened, and I definitely saw something under the wooden trails.'

'The Pukwudgies hang out under those sometimes. What did it look like?'

'I didn't get a good look, just dark and moving around. It had a funny, lumpy shape. It could have been a junk monster, but I didn't read anything about them making people mean.' She dropped the ball and it rolled toward the other students who were also practicing.

Cam went over to retrieve it and waved at the other students apologetically. When he returned he sensed, 'Has anything gone missing from the buses?'

'I guess we could ask around about that. I just feel like we're missing something important. Is there anywhere else you wanted to search?' Nora asked.

'Loads of places. What if we tell our parents we're working on a project after school and need to be home late. We could search for stuff while no one's around.' Cam wondered. 'I walk home most days anyway.'

'I normally help look after my sister when I get home, but she's going over her friend's house today. Liam's mom might not mind dropping off me and AJ since we all live nearby.' All at once, she realized she had been standing holding the ball awkwardly for a minute and Cam was just watching her.

Setting it down on the ground, she walked toward the bleachers to trade with Penelope.

'*Oh, yeah, I guess we could all look together.*'

Nora didn't have time to wonder why Cameron sounded disappointed. Penelope had already been heading towards them and took the ball.

"Wow, you really don't like volleyball," she said.

"Huh?"

"You were barely hitting it."

Nora hadn't realized she had made such a poor show of hitting the ball. It must have appeared as though she was putting in very little effort, since they didn't even pass it back and forth over the net. Glancing over to the gym teacher, she saw him chatting with a group of students and hoped her poor performance wouldn't affect her grade. She wanted to make honors this year even with all of the Secret Wing distractions.

CHAPTER 13

It was easy enough for Liam to borrow Cam's cellphone and arrange for his mom to pick them up an hour later. Cam would often play basketball at a park nearby before walking home, so his parents were used to him coming home late and Nora's mom would be asleep for several hours. The only one who offered no explanation was AJ, who simply met up with them in the glass classroom in the Secret Wing.

There was no sign of Mrs. M. or Mr. Walker and many of the lights had been turned off for the night. The hallway lights were automatic with motion-sensors, so it was not as creepy as the nearly empty school could have been.

"Ok, where should we start?" Liam asked.

They were all wearing their coats and their backpacks, since they wanted to end the school day looking as if nothing out of the ordinary was going on. Cam unrolled his map with areas circled on it while Nora flipped books open to pages about junk monsters and Pukwudgies.

"I have narrowed things down to these areas. Things have been going missing by the gym locker rooms, the lunchroom, and the library. All of them are by the back of the building. I searched any areas where something could easily be hiding, storage closets, unused rooms, but I didn't find anything out of the ordinary." Cam pulled his braids back tightly into a ponytail and pointed at sections of the blueprint.

When he paused, Nora took over. "It could be a junk monster made of all the parts of the things that are going missing, but I'm starting to think that might not fit. Something normally creates the junk monster, and we haven't found any clues to indicate that. Also, with all the things that have gone missing, it would probably stand out."

"We found that locket outside," Liam said, "and a junk monster or a pile of stuff would be pretty obvious outside. If someone forgets a sweater coming in from recess, the teachers notice right away."

"Ok, so it's not a junk monster, but it is going inside and outside the building," Cam pointed out. "I didn't want to mention it, but there is one place I didn't get to look in that's nearby."

AJ shook his head. "Boiler room is off limits. It's probably dangerous and we'd get in a lot of trouble going near there. We need to work through everything before we try something crazy like that."

"Good point." Cam sighed, but it was obvious he was curious about the boiler room and looking for an excuse. "OK, so where should we be looking?"

AJ was studying the blueprint. Turning it upside-down. Cocking his head like a curious dog. "I think I've found something."

All four of them leaned in to see what AJ was pointing at.

"There's windows leading to the backyard where we have recess. See, the lunch room, the locker rooms, and the library have those big ones." AJ pointed at the crude squares on the blueprint and squinted through his thick glasses.

Remembering opening the windows to get the smell out of the locker rooms, Nora realized how the creature was getting in. "We saw the quills leading up to the school. It has to be Pukwudgies." Nora said.

AJ and Cam glanced at one-another's eyes.

"Everyone has their rings?" Cam asked.

One by one they held up their hands to reveal matching silver and iron rings on different fingers.

"At least there's that, but Pukwudgies might shoot poison at us," AJ replied.

"So, you think we shouldn't go looking for them?" Liam asked.

"No, I think we need to see this through, but I want everyone to be aware this is dangerous, so if you don't want to go, now's the time to speak up." AJ said while picking up a lap desk and tapping on it to check its durability.

"I'm going," Cam said.

"No way I'm going to miss this," Liam agreed.

"I'm in," Nora said, "But if we find it, and it seems mad, we run away."

They all nodded and prepared themselves. Cam stuffed a thick book in his backpack and held it like a shield. AJ was wielding a plastic lapdesk. Liam actually took his bag off, deciding he wanted to move quickly, and Nora grabbed a heavy flashlight which was as big as her arm out of the corner of the room.

"Let's go to recess," Liam said in his most serious voice which always gave Nora the giggles.

They went out the door to the Secret Wing and walked around the outside of the school to avoid encountering any teachers or custodians who stayed late. Pine needles were falling and drifting to the piles of brown and orange on the ground. Before long they were at the wooden pathways, searching the ground for any signs of quills.

Clouds covered the sky, making it seem like it was growing dark already and there was a chill in the air to express that autumn was taking hold. It seemed as if they were searching for a long time before Cam waved them over to a quill near the boardwalk pathways. They were able to follow along the pathways on the ground, finding quills as they went. One after another, the quills led them away from the school and into the woods. Eventually the pathways ended and circled back around, but the quills were still going.

"This is Pukwudgie territory for sure," AJ said.

"Maybe we should have brought it a present." Liam offered, but when met with skeptical looks he shrugged and said, "What? I like presents. I think it would make anyone friendlier."

The trees were denser ahead of them and there were many dark bushes covering the ground. If Nora had been alone, she would not have had the courage to continue as far as they did. But, they kept following the quills, one after another, leading them away from their comfort zone.

Liam stopped to pick up one more quill, he was turning it over in his hand to examine it when Nora thought she heard a twig snap.

"Look out!" Nora yelled just in time for AJ to lift his lap desk.

Two, short, thin quills suddenly thunked into the top of the lapdesk. Luckily, they just barely penetrated through the other side, but the force of the quills knocked AJ onto his back. Cam ran up alongside AJ to help him to his feet, and a lumpy figure dashed out of a bush to charge right into Liam. Liam fell back and guarded his face with his arms. The creature clawed through Liam's sweatshirt leaving gashes with blood trickling down Liam's arm. Nora's stomach turned at the sight of the dripping red liquid. Without thinking, Nora swung the flashlight like a baseball bat, knocking the creature to its side and giving everyone a better look.

It was short, about three feet tall, and had the face of a wrinkled old man in a grimace. The expression it was making reminded Nora of Skip. Its little body had sparse quills sticking out at crooked angles, with socks, pencaps, and various other objects poked into the remaining quills or stretched across the little creature's belly. He was a menagerie of junk. It tried to get to its feet, but Nora held the flashlight above its head.

'*Don't you move, and you better not try shooting any more quills!*' she sensed to it.

The creature didn't move but glared back at Nora.

"Are you OK?" Cam and AJ were examining Liam's arms.

"I think they're just scratched, unless there's poison."

'*Did you just poison my friend?*' Nora interrogated the strange, little man.

'*Did I?*' he spat.

Then Nora raised the flashlight up as if she was going to hit him.

'*No!*' the Pukwudgie gurgled, '*No, I didn't.*'

The four of them gathered around the Pukwudgie cautiously with backpacks or lap desks at the ready. The creature moved to a seated position. Some of the collected objects had fallen to the ground around him. Erasers, a glove, a ruler. As he went to gather them up, he suddenly reached to his neck and grabbed hold of a red amulet which seemed very out of place amongst the junk.

'*Why are you taking all this stuff?*' Cam sensed.

The Pukwudgie snorted and spat out a big wad of greenish gook. '*Stupid question. My quills are falling out. You think I want to be naked come winter?*'

They all exchanged glances, unsure of what to say.

'*Why did you attack us?*' Liam said, holding his arms to his chest.

'*You came after me. Nasty human children!*' He groaned and held his head while rocking. '*Nasty, nasty children. Brought the one with the **eyes** to seek me out and put an end to me with your human metals.*'

Nora assumed the Pukwudgie was talking about her, since her eyes had an odd color that people generally remarked on. '*We didn't come here to hurt you. We just wanted to know why you were taking things. Do Pukwudgie quills fall out normally?*'

'*Stupid, lying!*' He yelled, '*You know they don't. I'm cursed, terribly cursed. All because of **him**. But, no, mustn't have been. He was so generous, gave me the necklace.*' He ran his fingers over the red gemstone on the amulet he was wearing as if he were petting a cherished pet.

'*Who did?*' AJ asked.

'*The boy! Don't play dumb. He came here, gave us sugar treats and trinkets. I was his favorite though, said I was better than the rest. Gave me the amulet, amulet of a king!*' He continued to inspect the gem lovingly.

'*Did he have a name?*' AJ continued calmly.

'*Why?! Humans, so obsessed with naming. Carlos, Carlos he said. What does it matter now? Haven't seen him in months. Must think I'm ugly now! Cruel!*' He suddenly lunged at Nora and grabbed the flashlight. Even though he was small, he was very strong. The two of them pulled on either side of it. Cam and Liam rushed to help Nora.

Meanwhile, AJ had gotten ahold of the necklace around the Pukwudgies neck. He tugged at it hard, and the clasp gave way. Before the rest of them realized it, AJ was running as fast as he could back to the school, holding the amulet. Liam and Cam were shocked, but the Pukwudgie let go of the flashlight and let out a tremendous wail before running after AJ as fast as his little legs would take him.

Fortunately, AJ had a head start, and the Pukwudgie was too small to keep up. They knew AJ would head back to the Secret Wing for shelter from the Pukwudgie. The magical door kept anyone who wasn't a Wyrd student from entering from the outside and the Pukwudge probably wouldn't think to go through the rest of the school to find him.

Nora, Liam, and Cam went for the nearest door, which was, thankfully, unlocked. Soon they were huffing and puffing their way through the corridors back to the glass classroom. Somehow they didn't run into any teachers who stayed after on their way there.

AJ was even more out of breath than the rest of them when he came around the corner. Holding the amulet above him, he leaned forward onto a desk.

"What was that all about?" Cam asked.

AJ tossed the amulet onto the table and sank to his knees. He sensed out to them, *'He said he got the amulet from Carlos. It must be cursed to cause him to lose his quills. I don't know why Carlos would do that, but it seemed like the only logical explanation. With how attached the Pukwudgie was to it, I didn't think we'd be able to get him to give it to us.'*

"That was quick thinking. Maybe Yeats can identify it." Cam said, "Liam should clean out those cuts too, so they don't get infected. There's some first aid stuff by Mr. Walker's office."

Liam took off his sweatshirt to reveal long, but shallow cuts on his arms. Although they were no longer bleeding, they were red and puffy. "I don't know how I'm going to explain this to my parents."

"Kind of looks like cat scratches?" Nora said, "But if we say it was a stray cat, you'll have to get rabies shots."

Liam crumpled up his nose and shook his head.

"Some dogs could claw you up when they're excited. Tell her my mom brought our dog to school to pick me up and you were rough-housing with her." Cam shrugged. "We gotta get rid of that sweatshirt though." He pulled an orange fleece out of his backpack and tossed it to Liam.

Liam caught it and thanked Cam even though Nora knew he hated the color.

After Liam cleaned his arms off with soap and water in the bathroom, they used the first aid kit to put antiseptic cream on the cuts before wrapping them with bandages. AJ seemed to know the most about treating cuts, so he instructed them.

Itching to get into the library, Nora had to stop herself from rushing in and yelling for Yeats. She hadn't seen Yeats since their encounter with Carlos, and even though she was practically exploding with questions about it, she was more worried for Yeats' well-being. She knew he wasn't a regular cat, but she was already growing attached to him as if he were.

She let Cam push the heavy library door open. The library had a very different feel without the sunlight brightening it. Instead, all of the antique lamps from a variety of time periods were lit. Even with all of them on, they didn't provide as much light as when the sun was high.

'*Yeats?*' Nora could not help but ask.

'*Naughty, naughty.*' Yeats was sitting on a table behind them, which they had already walked by. Somehow they had not seen him there before. '*As I hear it, children are supposed to avoid school, not stay after-hours on purpose. I don't suppose you cleared this little adventure with the teachers.*'

'*We didn't have time to,*' Cam sensed back.

'*I see. And what can I do for you then?*' Yeats appeared much more awake than Nora had ever seen him before. His green eyes were wide open as he stared at all of them without blinking and he sat upright with excellent posture. He sniffed the air, '*Attacked by a Pukwudgie, were we?*'

'*Yeah, for one, we want to make sure Liam will be OK,*' Nora sensed. '*I'm also glad to see you're fine. I was worried after you told us to run.*'

Yeats strolled over to Nora and rubbed his head against her. '*Worried? About me? Noh-Rah, it would take more than a shapechanger to get the jump on me.*'

AJ and Cam exchanged glances. Nora was starting to get annoyed with them since they were clearly keeping a secret from her. Making sure to put her ring in her pocket first, Nora scratched the side of Yeats' cheeks and he purred.

'*For the delicious sashimi, I will let you know that the boy will heal into his perfectly careless self in no-time. I do not smell any infection or poison in his wounds.*' He sniffed at the air near Liam again, adding, '*I must say though, you lucked out not becoming a pin-cushion for their quills.*'

'*That's the other thing we came here about,*' AJ dropped the amulet onto the table beside Yeats.

The usual disinterest on Yeats' face disappeared. His pupils grew so wide that his eyes were black as he approached the amulet. '*This is a magical item indeed. Cursed, of course, but a rare artifact. Where did you get it?*'

'*That Carlos or Fresh or whatever his name is, gave it to the Pukwudgie, and we think it made his quills fall out,*' Liam sensed.

'*Lucky that's all it did,*' Yeats sensed back. '*You'll need to put it in the drawer in Mr. Walker's room with all of the other cursed objects, of course.*'

'*Wait, which drawer?!*' Liam was taken back. '*I used a pen out of one of those drawers!*'

Yeats ignored him. '*Of course, I could hold onto it for safekeeping for now.*' Yeats moved his paw to collect it when AJ put his hand over it.

'*Tell us about Carlos and you can have it. We won't even tell the teachers about it.*' AJ sensed.

'*I don't know,*' Cam started.

'*I do,*' Aj sensed. '*We've been in the dark with all of this for too long. Tell us what's going on and you can have the amulet.*'

Nora had never seen a cat smile quite like Yeats was. He was beginning to resemble the Cheshire Cat more than a real cat. '*If all of you agree not to mention the amulet to the teachers, we have an accord. A deal.*'

Looking to her companions, Nora felt uneasy. She could tell that Liam and Cam felt the same way by their expressions. They were expressly told not to make deals with Yeats. Snacks and cat toys were one thing, but this was a magical object that they didn't understand. AJ, on the other hand, refused to make eye contact with the rest of them. He simply nodded to Yeats and they followed suit.

'*Very good.*' Yeats swiped up the amulet with his paw and rushed away with it. Once he was under the tables, they lost sight of him.

"Are you sure that was a good idea?" Cam whispered.

"You have any better suggestions?" AJ asked.

But before Cameron could answer, Yeats had returned. *'What is it you'd like to know?'*

'What is Carlos?' AJ began.

'That's one, you have two questions left.' Yeats sensed.

'What? You didn't tell us that!' Liam protested.

'That's just the way deals work,' Yeats responded without attending Liam. *'Carlos was a wyrd student here and his younger sister remains here.'*

'No,' AJ said, *'you don't get to do that. You know the intention of my question was the Carlos who gave the amulet to the Pukwudgie.'*

*'Oh, did you want to know what **that** Carlos is?'* Yeats settled down onto his stomach on the table.

AJ was beginning to grow angry as were the other two boys. Realizing this was all some sort of riddle to Yeats, Nora stepped in. "Hold on. Let's figure out exactly what we want to ask and how."

"This is stupid, he knows what we're saying!" Liam threw his hands in the air.

"Yes, yelling about it won't help. I think we should ask if Yeats can tell us exactly what type of magical creature Carlos is and why he is at the school pretending to be Maria's brother," Nora suggested. "But maybe we could word it better?"

"Ok, let me try." Cam said. *'Yeats, we would like to know in as much detail as possible, what specific type of magical creature the Carlos who was in the library with you today and gave the amulet to a Pukwudgie...is?'*

Yeats turned his head to the side and then sat up. *'That's two. Carlos is a faerie who can change its shape, known as a Changeling. Normally*

Changelings are switched with a human child at birth and they enjoy causing all kinds of mischief growing up in the form of that human with their family. I believe this one is particularly dangerous.'

"Should we ask why he's here or how we can protect ourselves from him?" Nora wondered.

"If he's a faerie, then iron is probably our best bet and to stay away from him. I want to know what he's trying to do here." AJ replied.

"How would the cat know?" Liam said before a sneeze took him.

Yeats glared back.

"I think we should probably..."

Cam's voice was muffled by the sound of an enormous, old clock chiming. The kids were startled, but Liam rushed over to the clock.

"What time is it?! Oh no, my mom must've been waiting for us for a half an hour." He rushed out of the library to get his backpack from the classroom.

"We'll have to figure out the last question tomorrow," AJ said.

Cam and AJ left to catch up with Liam. Nora lingered for a moment watching Yeats who was gazing up at her, his tail twitching.

'The Pukwudgie said something weird about my eyes.' Nora sensed.

'I'm sure it did,' Yeats responded, and Nora knew that was all the information she could get out of him.

She headed to the door of the library but right when she was about to leave, a thought popped into her head that she didn't even realize she was sensing out, *'I wish you could come home with me.'*

Yeats sat upright again and squinted his eyes. *'You'd invite me to your residence, knowing what I am?'*

Maybe she was overtired from such a long day, but she honestly enjoyed Yeats' company and wanted him to know. '*Yes, I would. I know it's not a good idea, but I used to have a cat, and she died. I miss her so much. It'd be nice to have a friend like that again. I was really worried about you, you know.*' As Nora let the door shut behind her, she could see Yeats' bright green eyes watching her go, but could not figure out what the expression on his face meant.

CHAPTER 14

Anxious and excited, Nora got on the school bus practically bursting with ideas on how to phrase the question for Yeats and what they would do with the information. The four of them had agreed not to ask Yeats the question until they were all able to be together for it that afternoon. The night before, her moms didn't even notice she had stayed late at school. Of course, Liam's mom was not happy about being made to wait, so she resolved to get Liam a cellphone to make sure nothing like that happened again.

Oddly enough, the thing Nora was most nervous about that day was art class with Maria. She wasn't sure how to broach the subject of Maria's brother or what had happened the previous year, but she was certain Maria could answer her questions. The more she thought about it, the more she wondered what the deal was with Carlos. Kimi seemed to think Carlos was nice, but maybe that was the real Carlos and not the Changeling. Why did the shapechanger choose his shape? She needed to know.

When the bus screeched to a halt in front of the school, and Skip yelled something insulting to the students about being slow as snails, Nora couldn't help but stand up and shove her way through to head to the Secret Wing. It didn't seem like any students were watching her as she passed to the side of the building, but even if they saw her, she would just say she was going to the Special Ed Department. AJ didn't follow her this time, since he didn't actually have class there in the morning.

Even though Nora knew she was supposed to go to homeroom, she made the decision to skip it considering everything going on. She might be reprimanded by Mr. Walker, but he would cover for her. It wasn't like her to skip any classes, but homeroom wasn't a real class anyway.

Pushing her fingertips against the letters on the cool metal of the large black door, she entered the Secret Wing and walked down the long corridor with flickering lights on her way to the library. Before she got there, she ran into Kimi, who appeared to be heading to a classroom. She stopped and waved to Nora, her bracelets clanking against one another. She had strands of pink in her hair and was wearing a turquoise flannel shirt over her usual anime t-shirt.

"You're here early," Kimi said with a curious smile.

"Yeah, I wanted to go to the library and talk to Yeats."

The smile vanished. "You know I told you to be careful about Yeats. He's a powerful faerie."

"I know, but he is helpful and I like talking to him." Without realizing it, Nora was almost at the library and Kimi was following her.

"I'll just keep you company then," Kimi shrugged.

Nora didn't like being spied on, even if Kimi meant well. But, after pushing their way into the library, Nora decided to make the most of it.

"Can you tell me more about Carlos?"

"Carlos?" Kimi pulled her sleeves over her hands uncomfortably. "This again? I told you about him already. He was nice to me when we hung out. It wasn't a big deal or anything."

"So you liked him?" Nora asked, without thinking about the implications of what she was asking.

"What?!" Kimi covered her face with her hands, "I mean, he was really cute, and popular. Everyone liked him. If it weren't for being Wyrd, I don't think he would have noticed me."

Seeing how nervous Kimi had become, Nora tried to move on. "Did he and Maria get along?" Nora thought about the struggle between her and her younger sister who always seemed to be whining and in the way.

"Yeah, they are really close. Maria has a hard time with him so far away now. The two of them were constantly laughing at inside jokes, kind of annoying to hang out with, honestly." Kimi said.

"Ok, what about the Changeling pretending to be Carlos?" Nora pressed on, knowing she had gone too far. Even though Mrs. M had warned her not to ask the older students about what had happened the previous year, Nora was too curious to hold back.

"Uh, I don't really know anything about that. I have work to do. I'll catch you later." Kimi backed out of the room, awkwardly bumping into one of the tables, before rushing out the door.

Shrugging, Nora felt victorious for getting to be alone in the library as she had previously wanted. She scanned under the tables and around the shelves. '*Yeats?*' But there was no answer. She wondered where a magical cat would hide or sleep in the large library. Normally she saw him snoozing in the sunlight, but there was no sign of him on the tops of the bookcases. After searching around the card catalogue and calling his name several more times, Nora had to give up. He normally appeared within minutes of her entering the library, but he was at least part cat, and they operated by their own schedules and rules.

Since she was in the library, Nora looked for books on changelings. The more information they had, the easier it would be to make their last question useful. She felt as though she barely scratched the surface when the clock chimed and she had to go to the glass classroom for the start of their Wyrd lessons.

Liam was already set up in the classroom with his notebook out and Mrs. M had made a diagram on the board about protections from different types of supernatural creatures. She told them the lesson would be all about common creatures they were likely to come across and the best ways to avoid insulting them as well as how to protect yourself if you did happen to insult them. Although they learned more about Pukwudgies that they wished they had known before their encounter, neither Liam nor Nora mentioned it.

They talked about helpful faeries who would clean or cook for people as well as mischievous spirits. Although many supernatural beings could be traced back to some sort of country of origin where you might find more of them, Mrs. M explained that they have spread across the world just like people, sometimes even traveling with humans inside their belongings. There was no mention of the lunch lady, and even though Nora was curious about her, she figured she'd learn more eventually.

Raising his hand to ask questions and jotting down notes attentively, Liam seemed to be the ideal student in the Wyrd lessons, even though he was far from it in his normal studies. Nora tried not to be too amused by this. When Nora asked about the boiler room, Mrs. M simply stated that it was dangerous and to stay away from it.

Not expecting a formal lesson that day, Nora began to realize she had less and less time to research changelings before the afternoon. She wanted to tell Liam about the books she found, but she couldn't risk Mrs. M finding out about their extracurriculars.

By the end of the lesson, Nora's head was swimming with new information on monsters and magic she never knew existed. Eventually, Mrs. M left Liam and Nora to their own devices in the glass classroom, but there were only a few minutes left until they had to return to their regular classes.

"I found books on Changelings. I think we should try to look through them before we ask Yeats our last question." Nora said quietly, even though they were in a soundproof room.

"That's a good idea. My dad said he'll bring us to the comic store tomorrow, but I don't know if Cam will be able to come with us." Liam said.

The door opened while Liam was talking and Kimi sat down across from the two of them. "I heard 'comic book store'."

"Yeah, we're trying to find out what's going on with the buses and the comic book store is near the bus depot." Nora explained.

"So, you're going to walk to the bus depot, sneak around the buses in an abandoned bus yard, surrounded by marshes, looking for monsters?" Kimi asked.

Nora began to worry that she shouldn't have said so much. Would Kimi tell them that they were risking too much?

"I'm in," Kimi said, "The other Wyrd kids used to leave me out of stuff all the time, and I'm sick of it. Besides, I practically live at that store. It's the only place nearby with discount mangas. I'll meet you there at two."

Liam grinned at Nora. They were both visibly relieved. Kimi was an older student who knew more about all of this than they did, and she knew the area better. She was also really cool.

They didn't have time to discuss any more details, since it was time for their next classes. The soundproof room made it so they wouldn't hear any of the school-wide bells, so they had to use caution and leave a little early. Nora's next class was Art and she had been going over how to approach Maria in her head all night while lying in bed. Her thoughts had kept her up too late and she was now feeling the lack of sleep.

It was hard to be drowsy in the art room with the massive, colorful sculptures and wall-length windows brightening the room. Maria was already sitting on her stool, her back a little too straight and her long, dark hair hanging down past the edge of it. Neither Mac nor Steph had arrived yet. In fact, the majority of the students weren't there yet, and, as usual, the art teacher was also late. Maria had arranged her supplies neatly in front of her already and was gazing out the expansive windows.

As soon as Nora approached the table, Maria slid out of her seat and did something unexpected. She rushed over to Nora and wrapped her arms around her in a hug. Utterly shocked, Nora stood stock still.

'I'm so glad you're OK,' Maria sensed. *'When I heard that thing got into the library with you and Liam there, I felt terrible. It's all my fault he's here. I won't let him hurt you.'*

Flabbergasted for a few seconds, Nora managed to take her seat. She had been worrying about talking to Maria about the Changeling all night and now it didn't seem like it would be as difficult as she expected. '*Why is he here? Why does he look like your brother? And why don't the teachers want us to know about it?*'

Maria sighed. '*I really am sorry. I'll tell you everything I know. I think you deserve it.*'

With how open and friendly Maria was now being, Nora felt guilty for having judged her so harshly. Kimi had told her that Maria came off poorly because she cared too much about people, and now she was realizing what she had meant. Scanning the room, she wondered if any of the few students there had seen the hug and read anything into it. The four of them at that art table had been getting along really well last class, maybe they just seem like good friends now.

'*Carlos and I were like you and Liam,*' she sensed, '*but we didn't know which one of us was Wyrd.*' Maria started.

'*About that,*' Nora broke in, '*why did you and the teachers assume I was Wyrd and not Liam? Kimi said it could be either of us.*'

'*Kimi is trying to be open-minded. You have faerie eyes. You can likely see through glamours—faerie magic. It's a rare trait, and very unlikely for a non-Wyrd student to have it. No one told you this? It was the first thing I noticed about you.*' Maria shrugged as if it were common knowledge.

'*No, no one said anything about it.*' Nora tried not to sound too frustrated.

Several more students began to trickle in and fill up the seats. They got their clay tools ready at their tables, but Nora was too interested in what Maria was about to tell her to follow suit.

'*Carlos and I shared everything. Since we were barely a year apart, there were no secrets between us and we hated the idea of one of us learning about all the Wyrd magic and the other one forgetting about it someday. So we found books in the library about how to gain magic abilities on your own. The easiest way, seemed to be making a pact with the faeries. It has happened countless times in history.*' Maria was able to sense much quicker and clearer than the other Wyrd students Nora had met. It made the conversation easier to follow, and she wondered how she was understanding so much information so quickly without getting confused.

Even though Nora liked Yeats, she had a sinking suspicion that he may have helped direct Maria to the information on making a deal with faeries, since he was a faerie himself. Was that why the Changeling had come to visit him? She wondered how else Yeats may have been directing her to certain answers and away from others.

Maria went on sensing with ease, even when Steph entered and started asking her questions about where the clay tools were. Somehow Maria was able to answer Steph while sensing something entirely different to Nora. Nora was in awe.

'*We found a book about contacting the fae and we tried to be safe about it. We made protective circles, we wore iron at the power site. The first time we tried, nothing happened so we tried again and again. By the third time, we must have done something right, because he finally answered us. We talked to him every day for weeks. He seemed nice, but he said he was trapped somehow. He said he would lend magic to one of us, we wouldn't have to live separate lives. Everything we wanted to hear. All we had to do was agree to free him from the prison he was in.*'

Mac ran into the room. He rushed to his seat and sighed with relief when the art teacher walked in seconds after him. Steph had gotten supplies for Mac and Nora, and Nora managed to thank her even though she was doing her best to listen to Maria's story. The teacher picked a few students to help her gather up the clay and distribute it at each table. They were allowed to work on whatever they wanted once again. Nora mashed clay in front of her haphazardly.

'He was tricking us, and we fell for it. After we did the ritual, Carlos said he felt different– that he knew he was the one without the Wyrd. He was acting strange after that, but I ignored it. I thought maybe it had something to do with the magic he got from the fae. He began doing things. Mean things. Getting the other Wyrd students into trouble in school, fights with each other, and even got us attacked by sharks. He could have killed us!' Maria wiped her eyes with a tissue and pretended to be sneezing to cover up the tears.

"I have allergies too," Steph offered to Maria.

"Yeah, I get them in the fall," Maria said.

'Sharks? How? Where?' Nora sensed.

*'Right down the hall. He convinced us to paint a magic mural with an underwater scene. There were fish, turtles, **and sharks.** It was terrifying. The hall was flooded. Luckily one of the kids thought to throw paint on the mural. All the fish disappeared, but there was still water everywhere. That's why school had to start late. They couldn't figure out where the water was coming from. Mr. Walker painted over the mural just to be safe.'*

'That's crazy!' Nora sucked in her breath and faked a cough to cover it up.

Bowing her head slightly, Maria proceeded. *'By the time we realized the Changeling had switched places with Carlos, he had already caused so much trouble. I went straight to Mrs. M and Mr. Walker. I explained what we did. They helped me to find my brother and bring him back. He had been in a cell in some other world for months. I still don't know what happened to him there. Most of the other students left, went to other schools. Some had been expelled and others just didn't want anything to do with the East Wing any more. There were only a few students the Changeling didn't get a chance to mess with.'*

'*Cam and AJ?*'

Maria nodded and studied her piece of clay as if admiring her own work. '*The teachers banished the Changeling using some magic from one of the books in the library, and we all thought he was gone until he turned up in the library yesterday.*'

'*What does he want?*'

'*We don't know. I don't know how he got back here or why. But, we do know even though he can change his shape, he keeps making himself look like my brother. Maybe it's just to hurt me. I don't know.*'

Nora could see that Maria was getting upset and the allergies weren't going to be a good cover for sobs. Also, she had barely done anything with her own lump of clay, so she decided not to press the conversation any further. She couldn't blame Maria and Carlos for what they did. If she and Liam were given the chance to make sure they wouldn't lose their newfound gifts, they would probably do something similar. Glancing over to Mac, she saw he was designing a large, crooked rabbit.

"What?" Mac asked with a smile when he saw Nora's attention was on him.

"I can't think of what to make," she said, which was almost true. She hadn't been paying any attention to her clay.

"How about a bowl?" Steph suggested.

Maria held up the vase she was now smoothing out with her hands. It was really well done for something round without using a wheel, and it was small enough to fit in the palm of her hand.

"Or a rabbit," Mac laughed.

"Is that what that is?" Steph teased.

"On second thought, make something else. I don't want competition." Mac stuck his tongue out at Steph who responded by flinging a bit of clay at him.

Even though Nora was nervous about the Changeling and kept almost losing herself in thought with everything Maria had told her, she had to smile back at Mac and Steph's antics. She shaped a tiny flower out of her clay, but it was flat and not very detailed. So, she tried to make a few more.

'*I am sorry, for all of it.*' Maria sensed.

'*It's not really your fault,*' Nora tried to make Maria feel better. '*I probably would have done the same thing in your situation.*'

"I really like your vase," Nora said to Maria.

Maria passed it to Nora. "It would look good with your flowers on the side."

The art teacher walked over just in time to hear Maria. She clasped her hands together, her green, flowing sleeves falling back to her elbows. "Well, that is such a wonderful gesture, Maria. I love that idea. Fifth graders adding to eighth grade projects. Once you're both finished with it, we'll put it on display."

Nora felt a little embarrassed by the attention, but the other students seemed to genuinely appreciate their collaboration. Although she always liked art classes, she had never been in one that felt so positive and free.

She knew she was going to enjoy that class and spending time with Maria. Even so, she wanted class to finish so she could tell Liam everything she had learned. They had a lot to think about. Her conversation with Maria convinced her never to tell Liam that only one of them was Wyrd.

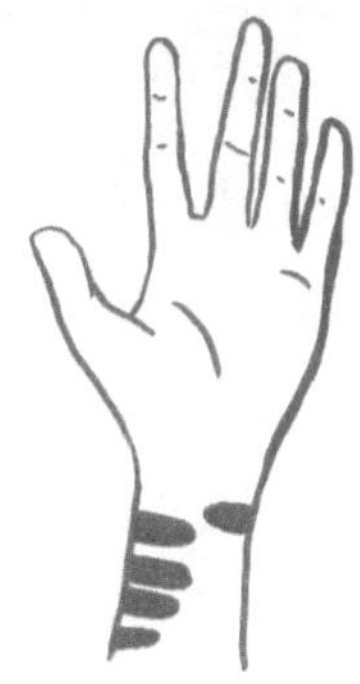

CHAPTER 15

At lunch, Liam and Nora sat next to their unfinished meals and went through the details of what Maria had told Nora. With the noise of the students chattering around them and the fact that there was no one seated directly next to them, they felt comfortable talking about what Nora had sensed to Liam.

"Why do you think he's still pretending to be Carlos? And why is he at the school?" Liam asked. He was furiously jotting bulleted notes into his notebook for the last ten minutes, but now he had slowed down to think.

"I don't know, but there has to be some reason for it. I mean, if you were a supernatural faerie creature who's been locked in a cell for... something awful I would guess, once you got out, wouldn't you want to go off and have fun somewhere?" Nora wondered. She popped a handful of red grapes into her mouth. They were sweet and refreshing.

"Yeah, I definitely wouldn't want to hang out at a middle school. I wonder what he did to end up in faerie jail?" Liam questioned.

The bell was about to chime when Nora realized something they hadn't thought of. "You think that Pukwudgie is still mad at us? Maybe we should avoid recess and go to the Secret Wing?"

"Yeah, probably…" Liam was in the middle of his sentence when all of a sudden he was covered in chocolate pudding.

The bell rang. Two girls stood over him, having just dumped their lunch trays onto him. Nora soon recognized the girls as Ava's friends.

"That's what you get for stealing Ava's necklace and then getting her in trouble, you stupid freak," one girl said.

Liam stared down at the mess on his shirt and pants, unable to think of any response. The lunch-ladies were on the other side of the lunchroom getting ready for the next class and students were filing out. The girls were already in the crowd.

"That's some classic bullying." Liam sighed. "Guess I'll be wearing my gym clothes the rest of the day."

Nora appreciated how Liam never seemed to get too down about the bad things that happened to him.

"I'll meet you in the Secret Wing," Nora said.

With that, they went their separate ways. Down the hall, Nora watched Liam do a goofy waddle, attempting not to get pudding everywhere.

On the way to the Secret Wing, Mrs. Stokes spotted Nora in the hallway and stopped in front of her. "Where do you think you're going? Fifth graders have recess right now." She had an angrier expression on her face than Nora had seen before. It was even more intense than when the girls in her class had started fighting. It reminded her of Skip.

"I have to go see Mr. Walker," Nora said.

"Oh really? You weren't in homeroom this morning and now you're skipping recess, galivanting around the school like you own the place. I don't know what your old school was like, but you can't do whatever you want around here." Her voice was rising to shrill heights.

Nora could feel dread creeping over her. She had forgotten to tell Mr. Walker that she had skipped homeroom this morning. Never having been reprimanded this severely by a teacher before, she wasn't sure how to react, so she resolved to stare at her shoes.

"I'm going to have a talk with Mr. Walker. You can't just come and go as you please. You know we have a thing called hall passes..."

Just then a commotion broke out at the end of the hallway. A group of students had circled around two boys who were shoving one another. Mrs. Stokes drew in a quick breath and turned abruptly.

"Stop this immediately," she yelled and dashed towards them, "This better not be about that slime again! I've told you it's not allowed. I've got a whole desk full of the stuff now!"

With how worked up she was already, Nora almost felt bad for what those kids had coming to them. It did, however, give her the perfect opportunity to escape. People were all acting so much more aggressively than she was used to. Even though she liked her new school, her grade school was much calmer. Something about what Mrs. Stokes had said was nagging at her. Fights kept breaking out, and there was a common element each time.

Practically running, she flew through the hallway to the Secret Wing and looped her way through the corridors to the glass classroom. How could she have overlooked something so obvious? It had been right in her face the whole time. With everything going on at once, she had just been too distracted to put it together.

Bursting into the classroom, she startled Cam and AJ who had just started eating their lunches. She hadn't expected to see them there, but she was glad to be able to share the news.

"The slime!" she practically yelled.

Cam and AJ stared at her as if she had gone mad.

"What?" Cam picked up the pieces of his sandwich he had dropped when she surprised them.

"The slime, that's what's been making people act all angry." Nora exclaimed, while catching her breath.

"What slime?" AJ asked.

"It's all around school. Like everyone has it, but the teachers are starting to take it away," Cam explained. "Have you really not noticed?"

AJ shrugged.

"Fresh er... the Changeling tried to sell me some the other day." Nora thought about it for a moment. "Actually, he was going to give it to me for free, but he was selling it."

Just then Liam strolled into the classroom in his gym t-shirt and shorts. He was obviously a little surprised to see everyone there. "What did I miss?"

"What are you wearing?" Cam asked.

"Long story," Liam answered.

"Nora thinks the slime is making everyone grumpy," AJ said. "Does this include the bus drivers?"

Nora hadn't thought about it, but they must be tied in somehow. "I guess," she said.

"Makes sense," Liam said while pulling his notebook out of his bag and flipping to the bus pages. "I've seen a lot of kids playing with slime on the bus, maybe the bus drivers are confiscating it?"

"I don't know, the bus drivers seemed to be the first ones being mean. Maybe there's slime on the bus?" Nora said.

"Either way, I still think we should check the bus yard tomorrow," AJ said while pointing at the drawing of the buses in Liam's notebook.

"I really wish I could go, but I have to babysit my cousins this weekend," Cam said and then took a big bite out of his sandwich. Nora hadn't asked why Cam wasn't able to make it that weekend, but she often had to babysit her younger sister while Momma G was sleeping, and she could sympathize with how much of a pain that was. "Hey, since we're all here, should we come up with the last question for Yeats?" Cam asked.

Liam and Nora exchanged a glance and then sat at the table with the other two. "We have a lot to tell you," Liam said while flipping his notebook to the rushed notes he had scribbled down during lunch. After they finished telling Maria's story, AJ slapped the desk.

"How could we have not known any of this?!" AJ asked. It was obvious that he was feeling a lot of frustration on being left in the dark. He nearly knocked his glasses off, so he reattached the cord to them that wrapped around the back of his head. "We could have helped or at least been prepared if something happened."

"We had our own stuff going on. Besides, the teachers probably didn't want to make Maria feel worse." Cam said, but he didn't seem too happy either.

"I feel like most of what we've been doing since I got here is cleaning up after the Changeling. Let's just call him 'Fresh.' If we could figure out what his plan is or even why he's causing all of this trouble, maybe we could stop him?" Nora thought out loud.

"Maybe we should ask Yeats?" Liam said.

"Why would he know the answer to that? I mean he knows about different types of faeries, but that's like asking Kimi what my goals are. She could guess, I'm sure." AJ had picked apart his sandwich and left a big mess on the table. He had barely eaten any of it after all was said and done before he got the garbage and pushed all of it in.

Nora could see why AJ was so thin.

"I think he knows more than anyone else. Maria and Carlos had researched everything in the library, so they may have asked Yeats for help finding the information, and even if they didn't, I think he just knows what's going on in the library." Nora couldn't explain it, but she knew Yeats had a connection to his library that surpassed any normal librarian. It was as if he was aware of where every book was at all times and exactly when someone entered.

"I knew it. That cat is no good," Liam said, "He probably caused this mess in the first place."

Nora was hoping they wouldn't jump to that conclusion. She shook her head. "We don't know that!" She protested.

"Why are you always defending that cat? Did he use a magic spell on you?" Liam looked Nora up and down as if he would be able to see a spell.

"Nora's right. We can't blame Yeats without any evidence. He's always been helpful—well, kind of helpful, to us," Cam said. "Maybe we should ask Maria more about how she got the information about talking to the fae?"

"You can do what you want," Liam said, "But I'm going to the library to get some answers from that cat. If he's the one at the bottom of all of this, I'm going to find out." Liam charged out of the room before anyone could argue with him. He was heading straight to the library.

The rest of them followed. Nora tried to think of something to say to calm Liam down, but she was never successful when he got like this. One time, when they were younger, they were at a farm and one of the geese was picking on all the other animals, so he ended up chasing the goose around the rest of the day to keep it from bothering anyone. He looked ridiculous, and they didn't even get to go on the hayride with the other kids. Nothing Nora said to him ever deterred him.

Throwing the library door open, which took some doing because it was a heavy door, Liam stomped inside. The plush carpet muffled his footsteps, which did not help what he was going for. "Yeats! Come on out here. We have some questions for you, and you better answer them."

There was no answer. They stood in the doorway for a minute before filing into the library to search around. Some books that had been taken out recently remained on tables and all of the lamps were still lit from the previous evening.

"Yeats?" AJ called again.

They searched under tables and in bookshelves, like Nora had done previously, but more thoroughly. There was no sign of Yeats anywhere in the library.

"This is strange," Cam said and AJ nodded. "I've never been in here for long without Yeats just appearing somewhere."

"Is there anywhere else he goes to nap or something?" Nora asked.

"Not that I know of," AJ turned to Cam who shrugged in response. "It's not like him to leave books out or lights on. Normally he keeps the library very tidy."

"He wasn't in here this morning when I was looking for him either," Nora said.

"Maybe we should ask the teachers?" Cam said.

Suddenly, a high pitched screech interrupted their conversation. Nora felt her heart skip a beat and saw the others jump. The noise continued and lights flashed. A voice came over the intercoms. It was a recording saying to remain calm and head to the nearest exit.

'*Fire drill,*' AJ sensed to them, '*we should go out the side door.*'

Nora covered her ears against the loud siren and followed the others out of the library. They walked with a quick pace down the hall until they reached the black, metal door which led to the Secret Wing. As AJ pushed it open, cool air rushed in. Liam grabbed his arms and frowned at his thin t-shirt and shorts. Each of them walked out onto the steps. The door was swinging shut behind Nora when something shot past her. Jamming his foot in the door to keep it open, Fresh stood between Nora and the door.

"Thought that would work," Fresh said with a toothy grin. "You kids really are gullible."

"What are you doing here?!" Liam blurted out.

"Heading on into the East Wing. There's some things in there I could use. After I visited the first time, the teachers put up magical protections on the entrance from inside the school, so that just left this one and I can't exactly open it myself. Thanks for the help." Fresh's hair was slicked back with some sort of jell, and he was wearing a leather jacket. He certainly did not look as though he belonged in middle school.

Lurching forward before anyone could stop him, Liam grabbed hold of Fresh's other leg. Nora could hear AJ yelling something, but in the rush of it all, she couldn't make out what he was saying. In a matter of seconds, Fresh shook Liam off of him like an insect. Flying through the air, Liam landed several feet away in the woods. Fresh then grabbed Nora by the wrist and pulled her up the steps next to him. AJ and Cam stood stock still their mouths slightly ajar..

"Anyone else trying to be a hero today?" Fresh asked, "Humans are so fragile. I could snap this one's wrist or maybe her neck. All the same to me really."

His grip tightened on her wrist if she tried to pull away, and it was beginning to hurt—almost burn. She didn't know how she would get away and hoped Liam wasn't badly hurt. If only she hadn't taken her ring off when they were searching for Yeats. Maybe it would have provided some protection.

"Ok, you win," Cam finally said, he put his hands up to gesture that they were surrendering. "Just let her go."

"Maybe I'll take her eyes before I go..."

"That's enough!" Mrs. M was around the corner moving quicker than she thought anyone with high heels could move.

At the sight of her, Fresh dropped Nora and fled into the woods. He moved so fast it was like a blur of the dark colors he was wearing. Nora plopped onto her butt on the cement stairs and held her wrist. There were red fingerprints where Fresh had grabbed her.

"Are you alright?" Mrs. M rushed over to Nora, helping her to her feet.

"I think so," Nora managed to say. She could see AJ and Cam helping Liam to his feet and getting the twigs out of his hair. Nora was relieved to see he wasn't badly injured.

"If you ever encounter something like that, you let it do whatever it wants, you hear me? It's not worth risking your safety," Mrs. M said. "What do I always say?"

"Safety first," AJ and Cam said in unison.

"Good, now I know you're new, but please keep your magical rings on and stay out of the way of that creature or any antagonistic supernatural being. You are too young for this kind of trouble. You are always to get yourself away from the situation and come to me or Mr. Walker." Mrs. M stopped herself from lecturing and looked down at Nora's wrist sympathetically. "Oh, I am sorry, dear. Let's treat you and Liam's injuries."

"Antagawhat?" Liam asked.

"Antagonistic — angry, mean, trying to start a fight," AJ clarified.

The fire alarm had been silent for a bit. Mrs. M brought Liam and Nora to the relaxation room. She then rubbed some sort of salve on Nora's wrist and on some of Liam's cuts. After wrapping Nora's wrist with a bandage, she told them to relax there for the rest of the day. She would make up excuses for their classes, since they needed time after their traumatic experience. Nora didn't feel like she needed to sit around all day, but she wasn't going to argue. She leaned back on one of the lawn chairs and found it much more comfortable than she had expected. She had planned to mull over what had happened and talk with Liam about it, but before she realized it, she had drifted to sleep.

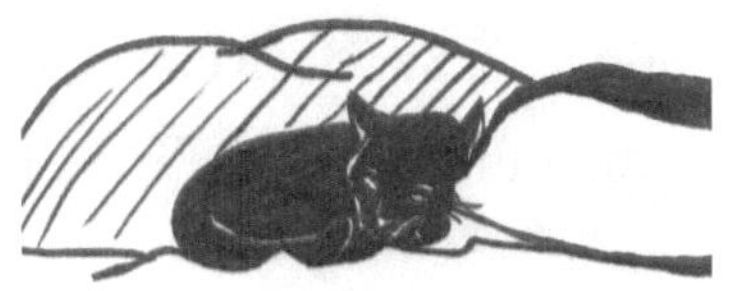

CHAPTER 16

Nora awoke to Liam nudging her. "It's time to go home," he said, "I talked to my mom and she said she'll give you a ride too. I don't know how I'm going to explain the outfit change for the second day in a row."

Rubbing the sleep out of her eyes and yawning, she lifted herself out of the chair. Her wrist was still a little sore, but it felt much better than earlier. Liam was still sitting in his chair, causing Nora to wonder if he was more badly injured than she realized. Before she could ask him, he looked up at her.

"I'm really sorry about what happened," he said.

"About us getting attacked by an evil faerie?"

"No, I mean, yeah. I should have just let him go by us into the Secret Wing. If I hadn't grabbed him, you wouldn't have gotten hurt," Liam frowned and put his head down like a puppy who had soiled the rug. He was still in his gym clothes but now his shirt had a tear in it from being thrown into the woods. It was obvious that he was having a rough time.

"It's not your fault," Nora said. "He might have attacked us anyway or maybe whatever he planned to do in here would have been worse."

"I doubt it," he said, but Nora could tell her words had cheered him up.

She held up the fist of her uninjured hand and Liam tapped it with his. They both smiled.

With that, Liam jumped to his feet acting as if nothing out of the ordinary had occurred. "We better not be late for my mom again. She's still mad about yesterday."

The ride home was much nicer in Mrs. Kelly's car than on the school bus. Nora sat in the back and gazed out the window at the passing trees that were starting to turn yellow and orange as Mrs. Kelly made small talk. She asked them how school was and which classes they liked. Nora told her they shared science class and she liked art. Liam borrowed Cam's fleece for the second day in a row, causing Mrs. Kelly to wonder if her son had a newfound love of the color orange. Liam groaned instead of answering, and Nora laughed.

After saying her good-byes to Liam, she headed into her house. Her mom was sleeping, so she crept to her room as quietly as she could. Dropping her backpack on the desk, she sat in a chair and unwrapped her wrist. Underneath the wrapping there were still red marks in the shape of fingers, like burns, but they no longer hurt. She had no idea how she would explain them to her family.

At that moment, Nora felt as though she were being watched. When she glanced up, she was met with two green eyes staring back at her from her bed. The black cat had made himself at home, curling up on her pillow.

"Yeats!" Nora nearly fell out of her chair.

'Yes?'

'What are you doing here?!' Nora asked.

*'I **was** napping until you started making a racket.'* Yeats sensed back.

'No, I mean why are you in my bed?'

'It's quite comfortable, though your sister's is the softest. I tested all of them throughout the day.' He nestled his face into the pillow.

Nora realized she could be at this all day. *'I mean, why are you in my house instead of the library?'*

'Why, you invited me here just yesterday. Don't you recall?'

Nora realized she had but didn't think Yeats would take her up on the offer, and certainly not immediately. *'I didn't know you'd come straight here.'*

'I was getting sick of that stuffy old library, and I thought you might have more salmon.' He stretched and became a very long cat for a minute before hopping over to Nora's desk. *'That doesn't look good.'* He motioned at her wrist.

'The Changeling attacked me.' Now that Yeats was in her house, she had to know if he was helping Fresh. *'Did you help free him in the first place? Are you helping him now?'*

She had never seen a cat gasp before, and it was a strange image. *'You can't be serious? How insulting! Maria and Carlos found the information on their own. I refused to help them when I gleaned what they were looking for. In fact, I gave them the same advice I gave you about the forest and the trees—trying to show them that they were too focused on one way of solving their problem. But they didn't listen and you did, which is one of the reasons I like you. Perhaps I was wrong to, if you think me capable of such foul deeds. Associating with that villain, blech!'* He stuck his tongue out of his mouth and shook his head.

Nora thought the more appropriate proverb for their situation would be that there's more than one way to skin a cat but assumed Yeats would avoid that particular example. She was now realizing that she had no evidence Yeats was behind anything. From his point of view, she had invited him to her home and then started accusing him of things left and right. *'I'm sorry, Yeats. I just wanted to make sure. I had a rough day.'*

'I will only forgive you if you scratch under my chin.'

Nora obliged, and he purred.

'Now that I live here, you will have to make sure you are stocked with the proper food for my highly refined diet.'

'Live here? I thought maybe you were visiting?' Now Nora had even more to explain to her moms.

'I shall have to spend all my time with you when you are not at school, how else will I keep you safe with those eyes of yours.' Yeats nodded.

'My eyes? Maria said they are fae eyes and they might see things others can't.'

'Yes, and they stand out like a beacon to magical creatures. Unfortunately, you are a target. You may want to invest in a pair of sunglasses.'

Nora almost shuddered as a chill went up her spine. There was an uneasiness she had never felt before. *'So, you're going to protect me?'*

'Of course. What are friends for?' Yeats added, *'As long as you continue to provide sashimi.'*

'But what about while I'm at school?'

'You're as safe as you could be at school. They might not look it, but Mrs. M and Mr. Walker have more tricks than there are sleeves. Supernatural beings know better than to mess with them.' He stopped purring and sat up to emphasize, *'And of course, that lunch lady.'*

Although she still didn't know what the deal was with the lunchroom attendant, Nora had more pressing concerns. She could hear her sister walking in, noisily as usual, and she was certain a new cat would warrant an ear-piercing squeal.

'I don't want my sister to see you until Momma G wakes up, can you lay low for a bit?'

'No one can see me if I don't want them to, even you, Noh-Rah of the golden eyes.' Yeats stepped into a shadow next to the bed and proved his words to be true.

It was a few hours before Momma T would be home and her other mother would wake up. She would pass the time concocting a story of how she came across Yeats and what happened to her wrist.

To her surprise, Momma T came home early and Momma G didn't have work. Soon they were sitting at the dinner table chatting about the pizza they would be ordering and the days they had. Emaline wanted a pair of shoes that matched her best friend, since they were both joining a running team. Momma T had a stressful day trying to photograph dogs at a dog competition and was glad to be home. Nora could not figure out the best way to tell them about Yeats.

"Um, I have something to tell you all," Nora began.

"Oh Nora-bear, your teacher, Mrs. M, called. She said you were helping move stacks of chairs and your wrist got caught in it. Does it hurt?"

Momma G said in a concerned voice. "I'm sorry I didn't ask sooner. She said the nurse looked it over and didn't think you'd have much more than a bruise."

"Oh, yeah," Nora was taken off guard. Her parents and sister were eyeing her wrist, "it's fine. That wasn't what I was going to tell you. Um, on the way home today this cat started following me, and..."

Yeats leapt onto the table and began licking his paw. *'Noh-Rah, I've been hiding for long enough. I'm hungry.'*

Emaline screamed with joy and clapped her hands together. Momma G and Momma T glanced at one another skeptically.

"So you just brought him home?" Momma G said, stringing her fingers through her short, grey hair.

"I didn't know what else to do. He's really friendly," Nora replied.

"He could be someone else's cat," Momma T suggested.

"No collar and he seemed pretty hungry."

"I think we have some tuna in the cabinet. Emaline get the tuna," Momma T said, while pulling up her multi-colored, wrinkle skirt to stand and assist her.

Momma G threw her hands up in the air and sighed. "Once you feed it, it's your responsibility."

Yeats took the opportunity to rub up against Momma G's hand and settle down in her lap. Refusing to make eye contact with Momma T, who was now smiling, Momma G petted Yeats gently and let him settle in. Nora wasn't sure if Yeats was trying to win over the toughest parent or if he knew Momma G's extra weight made her lap the comfiest.

"We'll ask around if anyone is missing a cat and make sure he doesn't have a microchip. Don't get too attached. He could belong to someone else." But as Momma G said this she gave Yeats the warmest smile. "I missed having a cat."

Emaline ran over with the tuna and scratched Yeat's head. He was the perfect gentleman, purring and acting pleased as punch. Nora's family fell in love with him instantly.

'*I'm not going to the vet,*' he sensed to Nora.

'*I don't think we have a choice,*' Nora sensed back.

'*I'll send a different cat in my stead, then.*'

Nora wasn't sure how Yeats was going to pull that off, but she also wasn't going to doubt a Cat Sith.

"What should we name him?" Emaline asked.

"I've been calling him 'Yeats,'" Nora said.

"Like the Irish author?" Momma T asked, "How intellectual for a cat."

Yeats turned, insulted and leapt to the floor with the rest of the tuna.

"Author?" Nora asked.

Momma T and Momma G both laughed.

"I think it's a fine name," Momma G said.

"I didn't say it was a bad name, just different," Momma T tried, making the same face that Emaline did whenever she got defensive. Nora thought out of the four of them, Momma T and Emaline looked the most alike, with the same tan skin tone and long brown hair. Of course, Nora also had a lot of similarities to Momma T.

Eventually, they all finished poking fun at Momma T and went back to discussing pizza toppings. Much to Nora's relief, Yeats had been accepted into their home without much debate. He had finished his tuna and was sitting on the floor with a satisfied, squinty smile, looking like the epitome of comfort, as only cats could.

Since it was a Friday night, Nora and Emaline were allowed to stay up late. All of them but picky Emaline enjoyed the pepperoni pizza that night. Their moms laughed a little too much at the animated movie they watched while they played with Yeats until it was time for bed. Emaline argued that she wanted Yeats to sleep in her room that night, but Momma G said they'd all leave their doors open so Yeats could decide where he wanted to sleep. Nora suspected that Momma G secretly wanted Yeats to choose her bed. Their previous cat favored their parents' bed. Momma T had kept all of the cat toys, the cat bed, and even the litter box with extra litter, which made setting up for Yeats much simpler. Of course, Nora didn't tell them that Yeats insisted on using the toilet like a civilized being.

While Nora got ready for bed, Yeats had already settled into her room. He had stretched out, relaxing on her bedspread.

'*Tomorrow's the big investigation,*' Yeats proclaimed. '*How exciting. Perhaps we should do strategic planning ahead of time. This is a first for me, I never get to be part of the Scooby gang.*'

'*Wait? You're coming?*' Nora tried not to appear too shocked, but she hadn't even thought about bringing Yeats along with her to the comic book store or the bus yard.

'*Of course, I told you I'm going to protect you outside of school. Don't worry, I can change my size to suit my needs. I can be as big as a tree or as small as a mouse; it's all the same to me. I'll simply hide in your backpack.*' Yeats pawed at a loose string on the blanket. He certainly had the mannerisms of a cat even if he sensed like a person. '*Now, the iron ring is a bit of an issue. When you are wearing it, it will diminish my strength a bit, but it will also protect you. I think it's best for you to keep it on until we find out what we are dealing with at the bus yard. I may ask you to remove it at some point, so be ready for that.'*

Nora nodded. The request seemed logical and friendly enough, but she still felt funny about agreeing to remove her ring whenever a faerie asked her to. Although she knew she shouldn't, she trusted Yeats who was quickly becoming part of the family.

Snuggling into her bed, and feeling the warm, soft cat purring up against her made her so content that nothing in the world seemed to matter any more. Even with the long nap she had taken earlier in the day, she now yearned for sleep.

'We should probably do something about that curse on your wrist tomorrow,' Yeats sensed while yawning.

'Curse?!' Nora's heart sped up.

'Yes. What did you think it was?'

'I don't know, just a mark…from a faerie…' Realizing how obvious it was now, she wanted to go to sleep even more.

'It's really not a big deal. Tons of things are cursed. Even a human without any magic could put so much negativity into something, it'll be cursed. We'll take care of it tomorrow, and I'll protect you.' He closed his eyes and nestled up against Norah's legs.

'I won't let anything bad happen to you either,' Nora sensed back, *'because we're family now.'*

Yeats' ears twirled back at that, but then his eyes became small slits and his purr grew louder, before they both fell asleep.

CHAPTER 17

She woke up feeling something heavy on top of her and overly warm. Her eyes did not want to open yet, but she pried them apart to see Emaline in her bunny pajamas sprawled on top of her to pet Yeats.

"Why are you in my room?" Nora asked through gritted teeth.

"Your door was open." Emaline responded without turning away from Yeats. She was making kissy faces at the cat.

"All of our doors are open."

"But the cat's in here. It's not fair that you keep him all to yourself," Emaline said matter-of-factly.

"At least get off of me."

"Move over then."

Nora rolled to her side, letting Emaline climb over her to sit next to Yeats. Yeats didn't seem to mind the attention in the least. Closing her eyes,

Nora tried to go back to sleep, but knew it wouldn't happen. Her mind kept wanting to go over everything she should prepare in her backpack for searching the bus yard. Extra clothes just in case they got cold or wet in the marshes, a flashlight and maybe her mom's leather gardening gloves?

'*Tuna,*' Yeats sensed, nodding to Nora.

'*You know we're going to get you real catfood soon,*' Nora sensed back.

'*Fish flavored,*' Yeats purred and rolled onto his back so Emaline could pet his belly.

Emaline exclaimed and made baby noises at Yeats. Nora tried not to roll her eyes at Yeats for hamming it up too much. In a few hours she was going to be picked up by Liam's dad to head to the comic store, but until then, it was Saturday. They would wake up Momma T and beg her to make pancakes. Later they would roll around on shopping carts while their moms were grocery shopping and try to get candy at the register. It was a typical weekend.

By the time Liam's dad's black SUV pulled up, Nora was already tying her shoes. Just as she was zipping her backpack closed, Yeats jumped inside and shrunk down to fit. Letting out a squeak at the sudden movement, Nora held her bag close to her when her sister asked what was wrong.

"Nothing, just almost dropped my backpack," Nora said.

Emaline shrugged and went back to braiding a doll's hair, oblivious to what Yeats had just done.

Nora rushed up to the car and hopped into the back seat behind Liam. Liam also had a backpack and was dressed in more layers than usual. He was wearing his usual blue baseball cap and a new sweatshirt. Nora recalled the last one getting torn up by the Pukwudgie and wondered if maybe they were getting themselves into too many dangerous situations. The red marks on her wrist would certainly make a case for that.

"Hello Nora, so you're all excited to play some board game at the comic book store. Liam told me it will take hours." Liam's dad, Mr. Kelly said, peering back at her in the rearview mirror, "Back in my day we only had Monopoly and Risk and someone would always get mad before the game ended."

Nora smiled back. She wasn't a fan of competitive games where everyone but one person lost. There were a lot of cooperative board games that were really fun. Thinking about them made Nora wish she actually was playing a board game at the comic book store.

Letting out a huge sneeze, Liam startled his dad.

"Allergies again?" Mr. Kelly asked him sympathetically.

"Sorry, we got a new cat," Nora explained.

"Weird, normally it only bothers Liam if he's near a cat. But we are in a small space together." Mr. Kelly continued, "Anyway, I was about to say that Liam can go ahead and give us a call on his new cellphone when you are done with the game."

Nora couldn't help but gape at that. Liam held the phone up to show her.

"Yeah, mom was mad about when she had to wait to pick us up. It's mostly locked, but it has a few games," Liam said.

"A cell phone is not a toy," Mr. Kelly said. "It is an important tool, and it is expensive, so you have to take good care of it and not lose it."

Liam mouthed the end of his dad's sentence as though he had heard the lecture multiple times. AJ was already sitting on the stoop at his house waiting to be picked up. He had slicked his hair to one side and his pants were hiked up so far that you could see where his socks went up to.

Mr. Kelly looked from AJ to Liam and Nora. "So, this is your new friend…OK. He looks like the board games type."

Ignoring his dad's comment, Liam opened the window. "Hey, AJ. Glad you could come."

AJ nodded and got into the car on the other side of Nora. He immediately pulled out his inhaler and breathed it in a few times before buckling his seatbelt. No matter how much small-talk Liam's dad tried to make, AJ refused to participate aside from nodding. He sat quietly the entire ride, waiting to get out at the comic book store.

They pulled into the parking lot, which had few cars for a weekend, and Mr. Kelly waved goodbye to all of them. He reminded Liam to call him or they would be getting picked up at six.

As soon as the car was far enough away, Nora said, "There's something I have to tell you guys."

AJ and Liam turned from their trajectory of the store to face her. When she opened her bag, Yeats popped his head out. Liam's eyes grew wide, but AJ just seemed curious.

"What is that thing doing here?!" Liam almost yelled.

"Actually, he's going to be living with me from now on," Nora said.

"What?! Why?!" Liam waived his hands in the air dramatically.

"I sort of invited him to stay." Nora shrugged.

'I'm right here, you know,' Yeats sensed.

"And he can understand us when we're talking, not just sensing, that's great!" Liam continued, "He's not a cat. He's a dangerous faerie! You have to figure out a way to undo it."

"I like having him around, and he said he'd protect me," Nora argued.

Yeats tucked his head back into the bag before sensing. *'Your pet is annoying, Noh-Rah. Perhaps find one that is less high-strung.'*

"Pet?! I'm the person! You're the pet!" Liam yelled.

'Really? And what makes a person versus a pet?' Yeats asked, peeking out of the bag's opening.

"Well, I'm a human and you're a cat. And humans outlive cats and take care of them…" Liam was trying to work out the difference to himself.

'I assure you that I am older than you and will outlive you by many years. And if by taking care of, you mean do my bidding, yes, humans are my servants when I choose them to be.'

Liam floundered. Nora decided to zip up her backpack. From owning cats, she had come to the conclusion that all cats felt as though they were the master of their houses.

AJ put his hand on Liam's shoulder giving him a small static shock that caused him to wince.

"Sorry," AJ said, "But, let's try not to make a scene in the parking lot in case someone's around."

"So you're fine with this?" Liam asked.

"Well," AJ looked from Nora to Liam, "I'm not sure, but what's done is done."

AJ made his way across the damp parking-lot, avoiding the puddles from the morning rainstorm. The day was chilly and dreary under the overcast sky, making them glad to be inside. Liam sneezed a few too many times before they entered the store, making Nora think he was hamming it up.

It had been a few years since Nora had been to the comic book store, and she now wondered why. The front was covered with action figures, there were shelves upon shelves of comics, mangas and graphic novels, and in the back were tables with board games and Warhammer minis. The atmosphere of the store was colorful and fun.

Kimi was sitting on the floor digging through a discount manga bin. Her hair was normally stylized with braids and colored barrettes, but today it was hanging loose over her face as she leaned down over the manga. Nora almost didn't recognize her, except that she was wearing the teal flannel shirt over her usual anime t-shirt.

'We're going to walk through the store for a bit and meet you outside.' AJ sensed to Kimi.

Kimi didn't show any sign that she heard him, but they knew she did. Walking by the rack with plushies, Nora wished she had some money to get one for her sister. Liam was inspecting a display case with cosplay swords in it, and AJ bought a dice set. Eventually each of them made their way outside to meet Kimi in the parking lot.

"You all ready?" Kimi asked.

They nodded and began walking in what Nora assumed was the direction of the bus yard. It would probably take them about 20 minutes at the pace they were going. AJ and Liam took the lead with Liam asking AJ why he needed all of those dice for Dungeons and Dragons, and AJ happily telling him all about the specifics. Nora was interested to hear more about it, but Kimi started a separate conversation.

"I can't believe you were attacked yesterday. That's so crazy," Kimi said pointing at the red marks on Nora's wrist.

"It *was* crazy. He wanted to get something from inside the school, but Liam grabbed him." Nora explained.

Kimi shook her head. "You guys better not pull that stuff today. These things are really dangerous. We're not superheroes or something, we're just kids. Kids who are good at noticing things." Her voice was sincere and a little shaky. It didn't seem as though Kimi liked confrontation.

"I know," Nora said, "We learned our lesson. It was stupid. Between that and the Pukwudgie...we're going to keep our distance from now on."

"What happened with a Pukwudgie?" Kimi stopped walking and put her hands on her hips.

AJ and Liam almost didn't notice and had to double back to where Nora and Kimi were standing so they didn't get too far ahead. Nora wasn't sure how to explain what had happened or if she should really get into the details. They were on the side of the road where there wasn't a sidewalk and even though there hadn't been any cars going by, the area next to the road was tree lined and covered in mud.

"We should talk about it later," Nora said.

"No," Kimi frowned. "What did you guys do to a Pukwudgie?"

"We didn't do anything!" Liam insisted, "That Changeling... Fresh whatever he is. He gave the Pukwudgie a cursed amulet that made his quills fall out. We snatched it from the Pukwudgie to help it out."

"Wow. Ok, so where's the amulet now? Did you give it to the teachers? They didn't say anything about it." Kimi was visibly annoyed and made no movement to continue.

"We traded it to Yeats to answer questions about Fresh," AJ replied as if it were an everyday occurrence.

"Yeats?!" Kimi asked in a raised voice.

'That's my name,' Yeat's little furry head popped out of the top of Nora's backpack.

Kimi's jaw went slack staring at the cat. They stood silently in a circle for a minute before Liam spoke.

"Right, we were going to mention that," Liam said.

"And this is all fine with you?" Kimi said to AJ.

AJ shrugged. Kimi looked from all of them to Yeats, who was climbing out of the bag to rest on Nora's shoulder. Even though he could change his size, his weight digging in with small paws still made it a little uncomfortable for Nora.

After giving Yeat's head a good scratch, Kimi finally sighed and said, "C'mon let's get out of the road before a car comes by."

"It would be quicker through there," AJ pointed at the woods.

"I'm not walking through a swamp," Kimi said, which was a relief to Nora. "With your pants hiked up like that, you'd probably get ticks or leeches."

AJ didn't respond, but continued to lead them down the road. Liam and Nora were now walking on either side of Kimi. Liam's shoes squished in the mud on the side of the road to keep them from spreading out into the road.

"Sorry we didn't have a chance to tell you any of this," Nora said to Kimi, "We weren't really trying to keep it a secret.

"That's Ok," Kimi said, "I'm actually kind of jealous you get to hang out with Yeats all the time. If I had known he'd leave the library, I'd have asked him to come places with me."

Yeats squinted his eyes approvingly from Nora's shoulder but didn't respond.

Liam shook his head, but decided not to vocalize his opinion with Yeats right there. In the distance, they could just make out an opening in the trees where a paved area interrupted the marshes. Bright yellow buses hid the skyline from view on the far side of a large parking lot. There was also a metal shack at the edge with a sign that should have read 'Bus Depot' printed in large letters above it, but some of the letters had faded into it reading, 'us pot.' Or perhaps some teenagers had purposefully scratched out some of the letters as a gag. Either way, no one had bothered to repaint the sign. It was no wonder they hadn't seen any cars on their walk, since there wasn't much out this way aside from the bus depot and what was likely an abandoned factory in the distance.

'I'm going to check the perimeter,' Yeats sensed before hopping off of Nora's shoulder and disappearing in the treeline. She hadn't realized how used to his presence she was until there was an emptiness when he was gone.

Just as they were walking into the parking lot, Kimi said, "Oh yeah, I saw Cam just before we left school yesterday and told him we were heading here. He said he'd meet us."

Liam and Nora both turned to face Kimi to make sure they heard her correctly.

"But, he said he was babysitting," Nora replied.

Sure enough, Cam came walking around the side of a school bus and waved at them. He was wearing a jacket with a basketball team on it which Nora had never heard of and he had a hat over his unruly hair.

AJ waved back and said, "I thought you couldn't come."

"Oh, right. My mom changed her mind and even gave me a ride. Pretty sweet." Cam said, but he turned away from them while he was talking. "I think we could cover more ground if we split up. AJ and Nora could come with me."

"Sure," AJ followed Cam towards some of the buses on the right side of the lot.

Nora pulled her flashlight out of her bag and picked up her pace to keep up with the two boys who were walking a little too fast for her. Shining her flashlight under the first bus, AJ and Cam went around the side. Cam's baseball cap was pulled down to shadow his face. She'd never seen him wear a hat like that before and wondered how he had tucked so much of his hair inside. It also seemed a bit odd that he showed up all of a sudden after saying he had to babysit. Stopping just before the edge of the front of the bus, she could hear the two of them talking.

"I'm just saying you don't have to wear your pants like that or look that nerdy," Cam said, "I mean, you look kind of ridiculous really. I hope no one ever sees me talking to you."

AJ was silent. "Can we just keep looking?"

"Sure, Splunker the Toilet Dunker, just dig into the mud under the bus like it's a big 'ol floater. Probably what you're into." Cam continued while laughing.

With his fists balled, AJ stomped by Nora to the next bus. Nora tried to stop him, but he stormed away so quickly, making it clear he wanted to be alone. As Cam came around the side with a smile on his face, Nora got in his path.

"What's your problem? Why would you say all that mean stuff to him? I thought you were friends?" Nora said.

Cam covered his face, "I don't know what came over me. Must be that thing we're looking for."

It made sense. They were searching for some sort of supernatural monster that made their bus drivers aggressive and everyone else get into fights.

If they were correct on it being based in the bus yard, then it would probably be worse here than at school. She did feel more tense than usual.

"I'm really sorry about that," Cam said, keeping his back to Nora, "Let's check the back of the bus. I bet it's close."

When they reached the end of the bus, Nora lifted her flashlight to scan the tires and through the rear window. She squinted to see inside the bus, but nothing looked out of the ordinary. Still, she couldn't shake the uneasiness she was feeling.

"So, what's the deal with you and Liam?" Cam asked.

"What do you mean?"

"Why don't you just admit you're dating?" Cam continued.

"We're not." Nora could feel her face burning. The uneasiness was becoming tight in her chest, and her anger was building. When she turned to see Cam, he would not return her gaze.

"Well, I'm not into fifth graders, so you can stop telling people I'm into you," Cam said, facing the ground so that his hat was blocking his entire face.

At first Nora felt embarrassment and then rage. Why was Cam going back and forth like this? He told her he would stand up for her if they were seen together again. He wouldn't embarrass her like before. There was this buzzing in her head that made her want to lash out, to just hit Cam to get him to shut up. Then, it all faded away to silence when she realized there were too many inconsistencies. Cam wasn't supposed to be there, he never talked to AJ like that, and he had told her he wouldn't embarrass her again. This wasn't Cam.

She took a step back, but the expression on her face must have given her away.

"Darn, I was just starting to have fun, too." Cam transformed into Fresh right before Nora's eyes. He was starting to look a little different, however. His ears had a slight point to them and his eyes were completely black.

Nora held her ring ahead of her. "Stay away from me!" She yelled.

But all of a sudden her right hand began to betray her. She felt a burning in her wrist where Fresh's fingerprints remained and her hand grabbed ahold of the ring on her left thumb and began yanking it off. Slipping onto her back in the mud, she struggled with her hands, one trying to ball into a fist to keep the ring on and the other attempting to rip it free.

Fresh had a large, toothy grin that was too wide for his face.

CHAPTER 18

Rolling onto her knees, Nora did her best to force her fist with the ring into her own stomach to add more support while her other hand grabbed at it. She had absolutely no control over her right hand and it was frightening.

"You really are annoying," Fresh said, standing over her. His tan skin shimmered in the bits of sunlight slipping through the trees. "It's why I had to get you alone. Those eyes of yours see through my glamours, making you a problem. Of course, I will have fun being you, once you're gone." He took a step closer. "I'll start by messing with your little boyfriend, Liam is it? He seems gullible. What fun I'll have toying with him, and then I'll move on to your family. You have a brother or sister maybe?"

Nora could feel the ring sliding past her knuckle. Tears were building in the corners of her eyes when she thought of all the horrible things Fresh would do to Liam, her moms, and her little sister. 'Help Me!' she sensed out to anyone who might hear her. She was too frightened and focused on her ring to think of anything else. The ring slid off and landed on the ground beside her. Covered in mud, and exhausted from fighting herself, all she could think to do was try to slide away from Fresh as he closed in.

Just when he was about to grab her, a streak of black hit him from the side with the force of a wrecking ball. Mud flew up around Fresh as he smashed onto his side on the ground. The windows of the nearby bus rattled as a terrible growl shook the ground. Before them stood a massive black cat, as tall as a school bus and almost as long.

"What are you doing here?!" Fresh's voice was shrill and his eyes widened staring up at the beast.

'Just looking for a snack,' Yeats responded as his large paw smacked into Fresh, flinging him high in the air.

Fresh smashed into the mud again and again, as Yeats pawed him back and forth. He was knocked up and down, back and forth, flopping around like a rag doll. There is no glee like a cat batting moving prey. When Fresh went limp, Yeats set his heavy paw on top of him.

AJ ran around the edge of the bus to see what was going on. He stopped. Adjusted his glasses. Squinted. Then went over to help Nora out of the mud. Soon Kimi and Liam were beside them as well.

"What happened?!" Liam said, looking from Nora to the enormous cat.

"Fresh was pretending to be Cam. Yeats saved me," Nora explained.

"I should have known," AJ said while retrieving Nora's ring, "I shouldn't have left you with him."

"It's not your fault. There's definitely something here putting everyone on edge," Nora said to try to make AJ feel better.

"Yeah, I felt out of it before the giant cat." Kimi agreed.

Yeats began lifting his paw and letting Fresh crawl a few feet before dropping it on him in typical cat fashion. It was difficult to watch a massive cat play with a person like they do mice. Of course, Nora always intervened when her old cat, Molly, toyed with mice or any smaller animals. She didn't think she could separate Yeats from the fun he was having.

Just then a slick, gelatinous creature about the size of a large dog slid out of the marshes at the edge of the parking lot. It had the appearance of a black octopus, but with even less of a shape and with tentacles that would only form for a moment before disappearing into its body when it wasn't using them. It slunk awkwardly across the pavement and up to the back of one of the school buses. It then used its limbs to pull itself onto the bus and ooze into the cracks of the back door until its whole body was inside the bus.

"Is it just me, or did that look like Inky?" Kimi asked.

"That thing in the fishtank? It's way bigger, but I guess," AJ agreed.

While their attention was on the school bus, there was a crackling noise and suddenly flames shot up from under Yeat's paw. He lifted it to his mouth and in an instant, Fresh was in the woods. He ran as if gravity didn't matter and he barely needed to touch the ground.

'That really hurt!' Yeats yowled while shrinking back to house-cat size.

"Should we go after him?" Liam asked, but they all knew the answer.

Fresh was long gone, and it was for the best. He obviously had powerful magic they were unaware of and even with a giant cat on their side, he was dangerous. Nora picked Yeats up and inspected his paw. The wound was closing up before her eyes. Rubbing his head against her face, he purred.

"You're a good kitty," Nora said.

'*You're a good human,*' Yeats sensed back.

AJ and Kimi were already peering in the windows of the bus before Nora could ask if it was wise. She turned her flashlight on to help them see. The closer she got to the bus, the more she felt frustrated and restless, like a black cloud had suddenly formed around them. This was definitely the source of the uneasiness they had been feeling. The gooky thing was crawling all around the bus. It slid over seats and across the floor, leaving a purplish residue.

"The slime!" Liam and Nora said at the same time.

"That's the slime that's making everyone mad. It comes from that thing," Nora finished the thought. "Fresh was selling it to people to cause problems."

"He was also there when I found Inky," Kimi said, squinting to see the creature through the glass.

"I think it's searching for something..." AJ offered.

Liam put his hand to his head as if it were so obvious. "Nora, it's like the raccoon. Maybe it's Inky's mom!"

Nora nodded at the plausibility. It did feel like a similar situation, making her want to help the slime monster reunite with its baby just like they did for the raccoon.

"Or another piece of the creature itself," AJ said, "we have no idea what we're looking at, honestly. It seems like the slime coming off of it might just be transferring its emotions. We should tell the teachers...everything."

"And then we can bring Inky back to its mom," Kimi grinned while patting Nora and Liam on the backs, "the new kids did good."

AJ returned an awkward side smile.

The creature appeared to have finished its search and made its way to the back of the bus. It began to ooze out of the cracks in the back door that it had entered in from. None of them wanted to find out what would happen if the thing saw them as a threat. In a moment of panic, they turned and ran out of the parking lot as fast as their legs could carry them. They were halfway down the road before AJ started breathing heavily and they slowed down to stay together.

'My phone says it's been over an hour, let's get back to the shop and actually play a board game before I call my dad,' Liam sensed.

'I have to change when we get there,' Nora sensed back while trying to shake some of the mud off of her clothes. Nora didn't want to talk about it yet, but she was still upset about her hand having a mind of its own. She wasn't sure if the others had seen her cursed hand grabbing her other hand, but she needed to make sure it never happened again. It was a terrifying sensation not being in control of a body part. She desperately hoped the teachers and Yeats would be able to help her. Earlier, Maria had warned that Nora's eyes might make her a target for supernatural beings, and Fresh had attacked her because of them. Even though the other students were there, sharing the experiences with her, they weren't being singled out as she was. A pit in her stomach began to form that not even the warmth of Yeats on her shoulder could seal back up.

The walk back to the comic book store seemed longer than the walk there. The sun was already starting to lower and the wet was seeping through Nora's clothing. With each step she hoped they were almost there, but all she could see was the long road surrounded by trees on either side and the swamp all around them. Swamp toads began to serenade one another, creating a continuous background noise.

"Here, take my hoodie," Liam said to Nora. His hooded sweatshirt was already off and he pushed it towards her. "You're shivering."

Nora didn't take it, but felt the warmth of it on her hand. "It'll get wet."

"I don't care."

As usual, she knew there was no arguing with Liam when he got like this, and she was grateful for it. Unbuttoning her jean jacket, she peeled it off and pulled the sweatshirt over her damp shirt. Immediately, she felt better.

Only one car passed by them on their return to the store. Although the driver appeared to be lost, he did his best not to make eye-contact with them. Eventually they were at the comic book store again. Nora used the bathroom to change into her dry clothes and got a plastic bag from the store-owner so she could stash her muddy outfit. Liam hung his hoodie on the back of a chair when she returned it.

AJ had already started setting up a board game on the table in the back. It was a strategy game where you played in teams against one another. Liam and Nora decided to be on a team together, even if the older kids would have an advantage. Time went by quickly, and Nora found herself enjoying the game. Yeats sat on Nora's lap under the table without any customers seeming to notice. After Kimi bought some Pocky, they loaded up on sugar, practically forgetting everything they had just been through.

Eventually, they had to call for Liam's dad and Kimi's mom to get picked up. Nora couldn't help but feel a little sad that their adventure was over and so was their time together.

"Maybe we should come here and just play board games again," Nora offered.

"Or D&D," AJ agreed.

"I still don't get what that game is," Liam said.

Liam made sure to plug Kimi and AJ's numbers into his new cell phone before they left. On picking them up, Mr. Kelly asked if they had fun. All of them, even AJ, responded without hesitation that they had. After sneezing three times in a row, Liam tossed his sweatshirt into the backseat, almost hitting Nora, and they laughed about it together. Although she was sad their adventure had come to an end, she was starting to get sleepy and her wrist was aching. A sense of relief washed over her when she waved goodbye and walked up the front steps to her house.

Almost hitting her sister with the door, she stopped abruptly in the entranceway.

"Oh, Nora, we're so sorry!" Emaline exclaimed and wrapped her arms around her.

Nora dropped the plastic bag with her wet clothing and returned the hug. "What's wrong?"

"The cat, we can't find him anywhere. We think maybe he got out!" Emaline blurted out.

Momma T came down the stairs. Long strands of her hair had escaped her ponytail and her coat was half on as if they had been rushing around. "We're sorry, Nora-bear. It's like he just vanished. We looked everywhere. We can search the neighborhood during the day tomorrow."

Nora instantly felt terrible. She didn't even know where to start to explain to them that Yeats had gone along with her. They must have torn apart the house trying to find him. She had to apologize and show them that Yeats was fine.

"No, I'm sorry," she began. Unzipping her bag, Nora opened her mouth to explain but ended up gaping when she saw no sign of Yeats inside. He had been in her bag during the car ride home.

Right then, there was a tapping and then a 'meow' from the front door. Nora automatically opened the door to allow Yeats to push his way in and rub against her legs and jump into Emaline's arms.

"Yeats!" Emaline squealed.

Thinking quickly, Nora said, "I was going to say, he got out when I left. I should have told you all. I'm sorry you were worried."

Momma T looked up at Momma G who was in her work clothes and shook her head. Momma G appeared as though she was going to say something, but thought better of it after a glance from her wife.

"It's fine, we're just glad he's back," Momma T said.

"We still need to find out if he belongs to someone else," Momma G pointed out, "but I'm glad he's back too. Gotta get to work. Goodnight my lovelies."

That night, Yeats received a lot of pampering. Her mom and her sister were ready to fetch all forms of cat treats and toys that piqued his interest. Unfortunately, it did not give Nora the time to talk to him about removing the curse that Fresh put on her hand or go over the details of anything that had happened. She was too tired to sense to Yeats while doing any other task, and she couldn't just sit there and stare at the cat who was basically ignoring her at this point anyway.

After dinner and a shower, she was ready to collapse. Hardly able to make it to her bed, she fell asleep almost immediately. It was a thick, dreamless sleep that only happens when you're overly tired.

CHAPTER 19

With a sudden jolt, Nora awoke to something cold and wet tapping her on the nose repeatedly. Her eyes opened to be met with large, green orbs only an inch from her face. Pushing the cat off of her chest she moaned.

"Yeats! What's wrong with you?"

'Your hand grabbed the pen and paper next to your bed and wrote something while you were asleep.' Yeats sensed, sitting beside her and looking a little indignant by the way Nora had spoken to him.

"What?" Brushing the crust away from her eyes, she tried to focus on what the words said on the scrap of paper. It *was* in her handwriting. "Why didn't you wake me up?!"

'I've been trying to.'

The paper read:

'Bring one of the deal breakers to the boiler room by midnight tonight or Cameron will be taking their place.'

Nora's heart skipped a beat. This had to be from Fresh. He had controlled her hand at the bus yard and now he was doing it in her sleep. The idea of him doing whatever he wanted with her hand made her want to throw up. Swallowing, she looked over to Yeats who was not even feigning disinterest. He was watching her intently and waiting for her to tell him what she wanted to do. It made her want to come up with a plan of action.

'Let's get everyone together.'

Nora jumped out of bed and quickly threw on whatever clothing was nearby. It happened to be a green shirt and beige corduroy overalls, which was not something she would usually wear together. Rushing to the phone, she dialed Liam's number without even bothering to look at the time. It was just before eight in the morning, which was early for most people on a Sunday. Mrs. Kelly groggily answered the phone and didn't bother to hide her annoyance when she yelled for Liam to get out of bed and tell his friend not to call so early on the weekend.

"Nora? What's going on? Why didn't you call my cellphone?" He mumbled as if he were half asleep.

"I don't have it memorized yet," Nora said, "It's an emergency, we need to get everyone together. Call AJ and Kimi and tell them to find a way to meet at my house. We can go to the woods out back and talk. Oh, and have Kimi call Maria."

"Hmm?" Liam asked.

Nora suddenly remembered the code word they had used when it was an emergency situation when they were young. "Turducken, Liam!"

He cleared his throat and suddenly sounded serious. "Right. I'll call them and be right over."

Surprisingly enough, it only took a few hours for everyone to assemble in the woods by Nora's house. Nora sat on a piece of foundation from the crumbling building where they had rescued the baby racoon. She decided to wait for everyone to get there before showing them the note and explaining what happened. Yeats sat beside her, occasionally hopping on a leaf or a bug. Liam was impatiently poking a stick into the ground when AJ walked over. They talked about the slime monster for a bit before seamlessly switching the conversation over to board games.

Leaves crunched noisily under Kimi and Maria's feet when they arrived together. Maria was wearing a puffy pink coat while Kimi simply had her usual flannel shirt. AJ waved them both over. They seemed uncomfortable to be there but found rocks to sit on.

"I guess we're just waiting for Cam then?" Kimi asked.

"I tried to call him, no answer." AJ said, pulling his socks up to cover the bare part of his leg from where his pants went up too high.

Shoving her hands in her coat pockets, Maria asked Nora, "OK, what's this all about?"

Nora pulled the note out and showed it to everyone. They looked it over and waited for Nora to explain.

"My hand was cursed by Fresh. He's been taking control of it, and there's nothing I can do about it." She felt sick saying the words out loud. "Yesterday he got my hand to attack me. And last night, he had it write this note."

Maria pointed at the note and said, "I'm the betrayer, I'm the one he's talking about." She looked over to Kimi who was spinning her bracelets nervously.

"Do you think he really has Cam?" Liam asked.

'*Undoubtedly,*' Yeats responded, even though he did not appear to be interested in the conversation. His butt was wiggling as he was about to pounce on a moth fluttering by.

"Why do you think that?" Nora asked.

Missing the moth, he paused. '*Is that your final question about the Changeling? You have one remaining.*'

"Are you serious?!" Liam practically yelled, "Our friend is in trouble!"

Before Liam could get more worked up, AJ cut in. "Yes, why do you think Fresh *undoubtedly* has Cam."

Yeats sat very still, pondering. '*It is not easy for a Changeling to appear to be someone else, they often need direct, physical contact—hair and blood. Most changelings are switched with a human child at birth so they can maintain one unnatural shape for many years instead of slipping between them.*'

"Hair and blood? But..." Kimi turned to Maria.

Covering her mouth with her hands, Maria said, "We had to add our hair and blood to a bowl for the ritual."

Kimi gasped.

"What? OK, can we all agree if there's hair and blood in a ritual, it's not a good thing?" Liam said.

Even seeing the humor in Liam's statement, Nora was growing nauseated by the thought of Fresh getting Cam's hair and blood. The others were obviously just as distressed as she was. Something else wasn't sitting right with Liam.

Getting up from the rock he was sitting on, he pointed an accusatory finger at Yeats. "Wait, if you knew Fresh kidnapped Cam, why didn't you tell us, like yesterday?!"

Yeats turned away from Liam, nestling into Nora's lap. '*Though I appreciate the high opinion of my vast knowledge, it is impossible for me to always glean what you know and don't know. You have books on Changelings, why you didn't try to check up on him yesterday is your failing, not mine.*' Plopping his head down, Yeats was making it obvious that he had said his peace and was done with the conversation.

Nora could tell that Liam was about to hurl insults at Yeats, so she knew she had to stop him. Even though Yeats had been nothing but amicable, she did not want to think about what a Cat Sith might do in retaliation to an impolite boy. "Liam!" Nora barely raised her voice, but he stopped in place. She wanted to remind Liam that Yeats had saved her from Fresh yesterday, but wasn't sure how to do it without making Liam feel bad about getting her hand cursed in the first place.

AJ stepped in again. "Yeats is right. We should have checked on Cam. Even if we didn't know everything about Changelings, we should have made sure he was all right."

Nora was feeling frustrated again. They needed to come up with a plan. "So what are we going to do?"

"Can we get hold of the teachers?" Kimi asked.

"I don't know how, do you?" AJ asked.

Maria shook her head, her long hair billowing out around her. "I've never tried on a weekend. This is all my fault. I should be the one to fix this."

"You're not going by yourself!" Kimi protested, "that's crazy!"

"He's dangerous, I can't let anyone else get hurt." Maria said decisively, crossing her arms across her chest.

AJ, Liam, and Kimi were arguing different points. It became a jumbled mess of:

"You're not in charge."

"Cam's our friend too."

"It's more dangerous to go alone."

Instead of raising her voice, Nora sensed the question that had been bothering her since she read the note. 'Why the boiler room?'

Everyone stopped talking and looked to Maria for an explanation.

"That's where we did the ritual to free the Changeling. There's a spot of power there or something. It's easier to reach faeries," Maria explained.

Yeats stepped into the center of the students. 'Almost. It's not a spot of power. It's a pathway, a place where the human world and the faerie realm meet. These gateways are all over the world. There are hundreds of faerie portals and ones that go to other realms as well. This is why the school has the East Wing. And an iron cage separating that room from the furnace. Only a fool, or a pair of fools, would go into the fenced area and then open it to unleash all kinds of beasts into the world.'

"Is that where you're from?" Maria shot back.

'How rude!' Yeats sniffed at the air and leapt off into the woods.

"Great, he could have been useful!" AJ said.

"We're not letting you go alone," Liam said to Maria, "You can't stop us from going with you."

Maria's face contorted as if she were going to yell something back, but then tears welled up in her eyes and Kimi put her arms around her.

"We need a plan," Nora said.

Pulling out his notebook and a pen, Liam settled back onto a rock and began scribbling. "Let's put together what we know."

Nora agreed. "We know Fresh is a faerie, so iron is our best weapon against him. We will all have our protection rings, but mine didn't actually work so great because of my hand...actually." Nora took in a deep breath, not wanting to admit what she realized. "I probably shouldn't go. If he can control my hand, that makes me a threat to all of you." Even though she could hear the words she spoke, she didn't want to believe them.

"Unfortunately," AJ said, "the note was written to you. I think he is telling you to bring Maria. If we all show up without you, he may run or do something to Cam. He's probably counting on your hand as part of his plan, so we need to figure out a way to fix that."

Relief washed over Nora. Not only did AJ believe there was a way to fix her hand but he wanted to help. Liam was already sketching Nora's hand.

"What happens when you put the ring on your right hand?" Kimi asked.

Nora slid the ring off of her left thumb and tried to put it on her right hand, but it felt like two magnets with the same poles repelling one another. When she let go, the ring shot about a foot away and almost got lost in a pile of leaves before Kimi retrieved it.

"Woah," Liam said. "My dad has an iron chain in the garage..."

Nora frowned thinking about being chained up or her hand causing a heavy chain to fly across the room and hit someone.

"Let's get back to that problem," AJ said, interrupting Nora's thoughts, "what else do we know?"

"Changelings can't help but cause mischief," Kimi said, "I think they feed off of it or something. That's why he caused so much trouble when he was pretending to be Carlos."

"OK, but is that why he wants to be here so bad? Can't he just cause problems anywhere? Why does he need Maria?" Liam asked without looking up from his notebook.

"He was being held prisoner for something by faeries and he needed us to help get him out. He put my brother in that prison when he traded places with him. And I opened the iron door to let him into the school, thinking he was my brother," Maria said miserably. She still had tears in her eyes. "The teachers had to go to the land of the faeries to get my brother back and they needed me to repeat the same ritual we had done just to find him. Then they did some sort of spell to banish the Changeling. We didn't think he could come back."

AJ chewed on his thumb while he was thinking. His glasses were reflecting the sunlight in a way that made it impossible to see his eyes. "There has to be a reason why Fresh wouldn't just throw Cam in the prison. All I can think is that something about the ritual you did connects you to him in a way that makes it so you can take his place in the prison, but maybe no one else can."

"You all keep saying 'Fresh?'" Maria asked.

"Yeah, that's the name he's going by," Nora replied.

"Wow, really lame," Maria said.

"That's what I said!" Liam almost laughed, but stopped himself remembering the situation.

"So, Fresh won't be putting Cam in the prison?" Kimi went back to the conversation.

"If my hypothesis is correct, but that doesn't mean he's safe. He could do any number of awful things to Cam, especially if we don't show up. He might want to make an example of him to ensure we do what he says in the future." AJ said grimly.

The other students looked at their feet, sharing the same worry and potential guilt for Cam's injury.

"OK, so we have to get my hand under control. Go to the boiler room, rescue Cam, and somehow keep Fresh from throwing Maria into faerie jail." Nora said, "And it would be nice if we could contact the teachers. Maybe if we mess this up, they could just go get Maria like they did Carlos?"

"I doubt it," Kimi said, "Fresh made it obvious that he will do anything to stay out of that prison. He probably has a plan to keep Maria there so he can stay here this time."

"We just don't know enough about any of this," AJ grumbled to himself.

"My brother didn't talk about the prison much, but I know it was terrible. He was different when we got him back. Thinner and there was this look in his eyes, like he was scared of something that wasn't there." Maria said softly.

"We can't let Fresh lock Maria in there," Liam agreed, "I wonder why he's in the prison in the first place and what the guards are. If we could explain the situation..?"

"Faeries uphold deals above all else," Kimi said. "If Maria and Carlos agreed to take his place, even if they didn't realize it, then faeries will insist upon upholding the deal."

"Maybe we can trick him into a different deal?" Nora said without fully finishing her thought.

AJ chewed on his hand more. Liam stared at his notebook. Kimi and Maria met each other's gaze. No one spoke, but Nora could tell they were all deep in thought, coming up with schemes on how to trick Fresh back into the prison where he belonged .

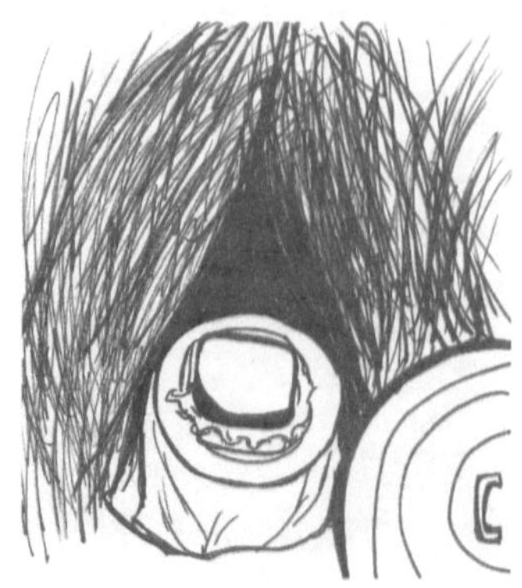

CHAPTER 20

None of them had ever been to the school on the weekend. It was a creepy, abandoned shell compared to what they were used to seeing. Dark trees hung over the building with long branches like grasping fingers. It had taken some doing, mostly a lot of lying, to get their parents to bring them close enough to the school that they could walk to it. Of course, the person who lived closest to the school was kidnapped.

Instead, they met at a house near the school. Maria remembered that Steph, from their art class, walked to school, and it didn't take much digging online to find out which house was hers. Using the lie that Steph was supposed to work on a school project with them, but couldn't get a ride, they were able to convince their parents to drive them to her house. There was some grumbling from Nora's mom, but Liam's parents seemed willing to drive them just about anywhere. When they got to Steph's house,

Liam knocked on the door and made up a lie to Steph's dad that they were selling candy bars for the swim team, which Steph's dad didn't want. However, it provided enough time for Mr. Kelly to see the door open before he waved and drove off.

Heading straight to the Secret Wing, Maria was the first to put her hand to the door. It opened with ease and they filed in. They had several stops to make in the Secret Wing, so they had decided to split up to put people on different tasks. Liam was writing detailed notes to put on the teachers' office doors, which he double checked and confirmed were both locked. He would explain what was happening at what time so that maybe the teachers could intervene if they dropped in at any point in time. They had tried their best to figure out another way to contact Mrs. M or Mr. Walker but they were both careful about their online presence, so their searches came up with nothing except that they were on the staff at the school and their email addresses, which they had made sure to send coded messages to as well. They were worried a school administrator might read the emails.

Kimi and Maria would go to the library to see if there was a way to reverse the ritual Maria and Carlos had done, since banishing didn't seem to work. AJ and Nora were on protection duty. They had to get as many protective items as they could to help them ward against Fresh. But, it wasn't just his magic they had to contend with, he was also stronger and faster than they were. AJ tried to think of a way to level the playing field.

"We could muck up the floor or make it really slippery. Then we'd all be at a disadvantage." AJ said while grabbing a few objects off of the tables in the glass classroom.

"What if we had an iron weapon?" Nora asked.

"They don't even allow potato guns at school, and it's not like we can suddenly smelt down our rings into a dagger or something," AJ said.

Nora's nose crumpled up. She wasn't even thinking about going that far. She wouldn't be able to swing a knife at someone anyway, especially if he looked like a friend. Liam walked in just as AJ finished armoring himself by tying a keyboard to each leg and holding a table-desk to him like a shield. He also had on a bicycle helmet from Nora's house. Nora had grabbed a garbage can lid and had strapped on her skating pads. Liam had attached a garbage lid to his chest like knight's armor and had another lapdesk for a shield.

"Are we ready to do this?" Liam asked.

"Not really," Nora said, but they all shrugged and headed back down the hall together.

They had the appearance of a group dressed up for a cosplay convention for some post-apocalyptic movie with a low budget. Once they got outside, they followed the growing piles of pine needles to the back of the building. A breeze caused more pine needles to rain down on them from the swaying trees which were now blocking the sunlight. As they stepped onto the wooden paths, their shoes made dull thumps beneath them.

Each time Nora was out on the playground, she felt as though there were eyes on her, which she assumed were the recess monitors. But, this time, there was no one around aside from the three of them and she had the same sensation. With a garbage lid as a shield and not even a stick for a weapon, she was feeling very underdressed. Of course, they weren't there to cause trouble.

Eventually they made it to the edge of the walkways, where they curved back to the school. AJ was the first to step off the edge onto the soft ground beneath. For such a nerdy-looking kid, he was actually fairly quick. They weren't entirely sure where they were headed, but it felt right to just keep walking straight back. If they didn't find anything after a little while, they would just turn back and try something else.

After walking for long enough that Nora was worried they might get lost in the woods, Liam pointed at a large tangle of thorns and weeds. The hedge was thick with a dark center as if it were hollow.

"The enemy of my enemy..." Nora said, thinking of Yeats' proverbs.

"I'm not going in there," Liam said.

"We definitely shouldn't," AJ said, "I have an offering."

AJ took a bologna sandwich out of his backpack and placed it on the ground in front of the dark center of the bush and backed up to the other two.

"How long should we wait here?" Nora wondered and after a few minutes she said, "Maybe we should have used a better offering. I still can't believe you two eat that stuff." As Nora spoke she was cut off by a thunking noise beside her.

Liam almost fell back as a blow dart struck the garbage lid which was crudely attached to his chest. He glanced down and then motioned to the others that it didn't go through. When AJ yelled for them to raise their shields, they grouped together and held their lap desks and garbage lids up over as much of their bodies as they could.

'*We are here to make you an offer,*' AJ sensed, '*If you are not interested in hearing us out, we shall leave.*'

There was a long moment of silence. AJ took a step back. Nora and Liam followed.

Then one of them sensed out. Its voice sounded shrill and aggressive in Nora's head. '*You, humans, dare disturb us?! You throw that ugly dwelling on our land and fill it with foul offspring. Now you come here, bringing your filth to our forest?!*'

'*We apologize for offending you. We will not come here again,*' AJ sensed, '*We only meant to offer you information on the whereabouts of the Changeling who cursed one of your kind.*'

Suddenly Nora noticed a small man, about four feet tall. His body was covered in quills and dark hair. Only his wrinkled, angry face could be seen underneath all of it. Adorned in something like a crown of twigs and dried leaves, Nora assumed he was their leader. As she scanned around them, she began to see Pukwudgie after Pukwudgie. They were surrounded by little creatures of varying shades of brown, holding all kinds of weapons from spears to bows and arrows. Some gnashed their sharp teeth together and growled noiselessly while others brandished their weapons.

"They're all around us!" Nora said, and the three of them instinctively went back to back holding their shields out.

The Pukwudgie who was speaking to them grabbed another by the throat and threw it straight to the ground at their feet. Although many of his quills had come back in, they were more sparse than the quills of the other Pukwudgies and there were still a few pen caps attached to him. The Pukwudgie snarled at AJ.

'*What do the rest of us care of this fool?*' the Pukwudgie with the leaf crown asked.

'*The changeling insults all of you by tricking one of you. It makes you look weak to others.*' AJ sensed.

Nora winced when AJ said that. The Pukwudgies took offense and drew closer with their weapons while growling and making all manner of animalistic noises. Liam grabbed Nora's hand with his free hand and squeezed it.

'*Our poison will make quick work of you, boy.*'

'*I do not think you're weak. We know you are fearsome, which is why we wanted to tell you the Changeling will be in the boiler room. You can take your revenge on him.*' AJ must have been frightened, but he was doing an excellent job covering it up. He had straightened up to stand taller than usual and he was sensing in a voice of authority. '*We intend to send him back to the faerie world, if you would like to help…*'

'*We will not be helping!*' The leader of the Pukwudgie sensed loudly and the other Pukwudgies cheered while closing in on the three students.

Nora held her breath. How would they get out of this? There were so many Pukwudgies and the three of them had walked into their territory. They had done exactly what the teachers warned them against, and there was no one there to help them. Kimi was right, they were acting as if they were superheroes instead of middle schoolers. Would the Pukwudgies poison them or skewer them and eat them alive? Fear crept through her entire body and she squeezed Liam's hand back.

'*You may go,*' the Pukwidgie leader suddenly said. '*It pleases us for you to punish the Changeling. But if you ever return here, you will die.*'

AJ nodded. The Pukwudgies cleared a thin path for them to walk through. Leading the way through snarling, spikey creatures with angry faces and sharp weapons, AJ kept walking without glimpsing behind him or saying a word until they reached the wooden walkways. But Nora turned her head to see the leader of the Pukwudgies happily munching on the bologna sandwich.

"Well, that could have gone better," Liam said, climbing onto the platforms.

"Could have gone worse too. We knew it was a longshot. I hope Maria and Kimi did better than we did." AJ pulled the lapdesks off of his arms while they headed back to the school.

"Good thing for this garbage lid," Liam tapped his chest next to the dart that was stuck in the thick plastic.

Nora wondered if they had actually been aiming for the armor to frighten them away. By the way the Pukwudgie was gobbling down the sandwich, she would think he was pleased with the offering. Trying not to be too let down by the lack of success, Nora opened the door to the Secret Wing and the three of them went straight to the library.

She wondered again if she would ever have a chance to really examine all of the carvings on the big, wooden door when they pushed their way into the library. Light was shining through the glass dome on the ceiling directly onto the pile of books on the floor. Kimi and Maria were sitting amongst the pile, talking animatedly to one another.

"It won't work," Kimi was saying.

"You don't know that. We have to try!" Maria was arguing.

Tossing his garbage lid to the floor, Liam made sure Maria and Kimi could see the dart sticking out of the center.

"I take it things didn't go well?" Kimi asked.

All of them shook their heads and sat down on the floor to join Kimi and Maria with their stack of books.

"We're not doing much better," Kimi said.

"That's not true," Maria argued., "We found a ritual to switch places with Fresh once, forever. I would just have to do it from the prison…"

"Out of the question," Kimi said. "Not only do we know nothing about the prison or what they might do to you there, meaning we don't know if you'd be able to do the ritual from there. Fresh probably has something up his sleeve to make sure you stay there this time."

Both girls had pulled their hair back tightly and rolled up their sleeves. It was obvious they had been arguing over the details for some time.

"So you have a better idea?" Maria asked.

"Maybe we could make someone look like Maria?" Liam suggested.

AJ shook his head, "I don't think that would work. Fresh probably can tell who he has a deal with. Even if he couldn't, he's an expert at changing his appearance with magic and probably knows what to look for. He had me fooled as Cam."

"I could see through it," Nora said, "because of my eyes. That's why he cursed me in the first place."

No one spoke for a minute. Liam's eyebrows rose sympathetically.

"We're running out of time," Maria said, "Our parents are going to come looking for us in a few hours."

"Maybe we should wait as long as we can, in case the teachers come," Kimi suggested.

Maria shook her head. "No, I've made up my mind. If we don't figure something else out in the next half hour, I'm going with my plan. Even if it doesn't work, at least Cam and all of you will be safe."

"Assuming he hasn't done something to Cam already," AJ shrugged.

The rest of them didn't want to think about that possibility. Even if Fresh seemed like he was capable of any number of terrible things, they were holding onto the hope that maybe he would leave Cam alone at least until after midnight.

Anxiously, they all made a search of the library. They decided to pursue charms or spells in sections that weren't just about faeries, because there was no reason to rule out other kinds of lore. Even though they separated into different sections, it still seemed as though their search was too big and too random. They would need a lot of luck to fall onto the right spell, and after twenty minutes, it was clear that was not happening.

"Maybe we're overthinking things?" AJ said from atop a ladder while thumbing through a particularly dusty book. He slipped on the rungs and almost fell a few feet before catching hold of one of the rungs and lowering himself to the floor. "The way to the faerie land is through an iron gate. If we can just trap Fresh in there, we can wait for the teachers to take care of him."

"The trouble would be getting just him in there without the rest of us." Kimi said.

"I think I have an idea," said Nora.

CHAPTER 21

The boiler room wasn't what Nora expected. She had pictured an old, rusty room with peeling paint and dust-covered walls—ill-cared for and creepy, like the final scene out of a horror movie where you couldn't tell if it was old red paint or blood thrown about and strange clanking noises masked the killer's entrance. Instead, it was very clean. The floor was cement, but it was painted a pale grey and the walls were blue. The furnace was a sizable, green machine with dials and tubes connecting it to the vents. It was making a loud whirring noise, but in an almost pleasant way that could help someone fall asleep. The adjoining room was gated in with iron bars like a jailhouse. But, it was small, like the size of a coat room, and was also very clean.

Fluorescent lights shone overhead, bright as day. Since the two rooms were so bare and clean, it would have been very difficult to hide anyone or anything in them. Kimi, Nora, AJ and Liam knew they were the only ones there.

Nora could vaguely feel her pulse in her arm and hoped they had not tied it up too tightly. In an attempt to keep her hand from being of any use to Fresh, they had bound it with gauze, duct tape, and pretty much anything they could get their hands on right away. The result was a big, goofy looking ball of junk on Nora's arm.

"Does he expect us to come at midnight?" Kimi asked, "Because there's no way my mom would let me. Tomorrow's a school day too."

But, just as she was saying this, the door opened. Fresh, who now had Carlos' features again, shuffled in, holding Cam by the hair. He was wearing a brand new striped t-shirt and khakis and his sneakers were bright white too. Cam, on the other hand, looked like he had been rolled through the mud several times. He had a gag over his mouth and his hands were tied together with some sort of fabric. There was a trickle of dried blood on his eyebrow as if it had been split. He tried to sense something to the group, but before he could, Fresh yanked him by the hair, hard. Cam winced and stopped.

'None of that,' Fresh sensed. 'It appears as though one is missing from your little group. It would be a shame for Cam if you intend to waste my time.'

'Maria's coming,' Nora said, 'but first we have to be sure that's really Cam and you haven't done any bad spells to him.' Without thinking, she motioned with her hand that they had bound up, so it was a goofy, comical gesture.

Fresh grinned at Nora, exposing his sharp teeth once again. 'Use your eyes and have a good look then.'

'We have to be sure,' AJ sensed.

"For all we know you cut his tongue out," Liam said while shifting the weight of his backpack on his shoulders.

Nora walked into the small room. Now that she was inside of it, she could see that there was something off about the back wall. It was as if it was moving in spirals. Blinking her eyes, she made up her mind to stay as far away from that wall as she could while she continued with the plan. *'I would like to be with him alone in here, so that I know you won't be doing magic on him.'*

Immediately Fresh squinted his eyes as if he was on to their plan. But, after a moment, he shrugged and kicked Cam in with Nora. *'Remember Cameron, if you say or sense something I don't appreciate, I can just hurt one of your friends out here.'*

Closing the gate, Nora glanced back at her friends on the other side. She was now protected from Fresh, but even with their iron rings, he could still probably do something to them. Nora helped Cameron up and removed the gag from his mouth. He coughed a little, and she could see his tongue was still intact. Looking him over, she could tell that the cut on his eyebrow was very small and aside from some bumps and bruises, he didn't appear to have any major injuries. She checked his pockets, but they were empty. She inspected his arms and legs for magical runes or curse marks like hers, but there was nothing on Cam that appeared out of the ordinary.

'What were you in fairy jail for anyway?' AJ asked Fresh.

He didn't take his focus away from Cam and Nora, but replied, *'Wouldn't you like to know.'*

'I bet they put him in there because he's ugly. That's why he has to make himself look like Carlos.' Kimi sensed and AJ laughed.

The distraction worked for a second when Fresh glared at Kimi. '*Oh Kimi, are you still upset the real Carlos didn't pay any attention to you?* **Notice me senpai!** *Pathetic.*'

That seemed to strike a nerve, because Kimi's face went red. AJ stepped up to defend Kimi, but couldn't think of anything to say. Liam sneezed from behind Fresh but remained next to the door leading out of the room as if he were ready to run away at a moment's notice.

"Are you OK?" Nora leaned down and took Cam's hand. She slid her iron ring onto his finger as subtly as she could with one hand.

"I think so," Cam said, "but you can't seriously be letting him take Maria?"

"Ahem," Fresh cleared his throat. He turned back to Nora and Cam. 'Did I not make myself clear?' He held his hands above AJ and Kimi menacingly.

"It doesn't look like a trick," Nora said.

'*Of course not. Now tell Maria to come here so we can finish this.*' Fresh said, balling his fists impatiently.

'*We will, but first you must make a deal with us,*' Nora sensed.

'*Why should I? Maybe I should just take all of you hostage and wait for her to come?*' Fresh smiled threateningly.

'*You could, but I'm guessing the iron rings we have will make things annoying for you. The whole thing would be an inconvenience, really. The deal is that once Maria gets here, you let the rest of us go, unharmed.*' Nora sensed.

'*Fine, deal,*' Fresh sensed back quickly.

Nora was still holding Cam's hand. He was watching her for any clues as to what they were doing. She pushed open the iron gate with her balled hand and walked with Cam to the edge of the little room. Fresh moved to grab Cam when Liam burst forward.

"Turducken!" Liam yelled.

Nora pushed Cam as hard as she could to the ground. Meanwhile, Yeats flew out of Liam's backpack and grew in size. His furry ears poked between two pipes on the ceiling and his huge paw struck out at Fresh, knocking him over Nora who was now on her hands and knees to help him trip. But, Yeats had actually swatted Fresh so hard he went flying over Nora into the small room. As Nora and Cam slid out of the way, Kimi slammed the iron gate shut.

Unfortunately, just before the latch connected, Nora felt pain shooting up through her entire arm. She had, unwittingly, shoved her hand, balled up in tape, into the mechanism, stopping the gate from closing all the way. Before she had any time to think, Fresh had already grabbed her, dragging her into the cage and kicking it shut. He was now holding her, with his arm over her shoulder while gasping for breath, since Yeats had knocked the wind out of him.

'*I'm impressed. Nice try,*' Fresh sensed.

Nora tried to push herself away, but Fresh tightened his grip on her. His fingers dug into her shoulder painfully causing her to yelp. Yeats growled so fiercely that it echoed through the pipes and shook the room.

'*Oops, looks like this iron cage is protecting us from you now, kitty kitty.*' Fresh sensed, over-enunciating each word to show how angry he was. '*And someone is missing her ring. Now, this is how it is going to work. You will bring Maria here at once or I will throw golden-eyes into the fae realm. She will likely be devoured by something within minutes.*'

'*You'd lose the only thing you'd have to bargain with. And we could just wait for Mrs. M and Mr. Walker to come deal with you.*' AJ sensed.

'*Then I would definitely throw her in, out of spite,*' Fresh shrugged and backed towards the wall.

There was a dizzying sensation, where Nora felt like the room was spinning. She knew it was because they were closer to the wall. She now felt really stupid for giving her ring to Cam. It was supposed to keep Fresh from taking Cam back as a hostage.

'*Enough!*' Maria threw the door open and walked in. She was wearing her coat and backpack as if she had been ready to leave school. Her hands were on her hips and her long hair was pulled back in a tight braid. '*I won't let you hurt her or anyone else. This is my mess, and I will clean it up.*'

A wider grin than ever before took over Fresh's face. He laughed a high-pitched nervous laugh. '*Finally. Come in here and take her place then.*'

'*I will, but only after you make another agreement with me,*' Maria sensed.

"Don't do this!" Kimi yelled.

"We can figure something else out," AJ said.

"I have made up my mind. Tell the teachers what happened to me," she said.

'*All of you with these agreements. I should point out that I have your friend and don't have to agree to anything, but I'm curious. What is it?*' Fresh asked.

'*I will go through the portal, into the faerie world, if you agree to leave the school and never return.*' Maria sensed.

'*Fine...*'

Maria continued, '*I am not finished. If you return to the school, for any reason, you must give up the agreement you had with my brother and me and return to the prison yourself.*'

Fresh put his hand on his chin, contemplating. While he did this, he loosened his grip on Nora. She took in a deep breath.

'*It is the only way I know my friends will be safe,*' Maria explained.

Fresh shrugged. '*Fine, I accept. With the stipulation that the cat stays out of all of this. I will leave and never return to this stupid school. Why would I want to be here anyway?*'

Yeats shrunk down to the size of a large dog, while the other students tried to tell Maria to stop. Nora was devastated. She felt like the whole plan was ruined and it was her fault. Ignoring the pleas of her friends, Maria went to the gate and opened it. As she entered the small room, Fresh walked up to her, still holding Nora to him.

'*You won't be needing this,*' He ripped the backpack off of Maria and tossed it heavily to the floor. '*Even if you tried to reverse the ritual from there, it wouldn't work. And, the jailers have upped the security, so they will be keeping you in this time, and the teachers won't be getting you out. An agreement is an agreement.*'

Maria had tears in her eyes. She obviously hadn't expected Fresh to remove her backpack. Fresh backed out of the opening in the gate and motioned with his head for her to continue to the wall. She walked forward with her hands out. If she was expecting to touch the wall's surface, she was disappointed. Instead, she kept walking forward as if the wall was not there until she vanished and the wall remained. Nora could see the spirals spin faster until Maria was pulled in by them.

'*Well, that was easy enough,*' Fresh threw Nora to her friends. '*Yeats, if you try to stop me, I'll use the curse to remove Nora's hand from her wrist.*'

Liam and Cam caught Nora before she could fall back. Yeats growled but remained by Nora's side.

'*Goodbye, suckers,*' Fresh said.

All of them stood watching him walk out, knowing there was nothing they could do to stop him. He was stronger than they were and more powerful in every way. If Yeats intervened, it would injure Nora and wouldn't get Maria back. He had won. They thought they were clever enough to stop him, but they were just a group of kids after all. The boiler room door shut behind him, and just like that, Fresh was gone.

"I'm sorry," Cam said, "I wanted to tell you all that he made it so Maria will be met by guards once she walks through. They are probably bringing her to a cell already. If I hadn't gotten caught by him, this wouldn't have happened." He sat down on the cement floor and hung his head over his knees.

The others joined him on the floor, sitting in a small circle. Kimi had tears in her eyes and AJ was mouthing something as if going over what to say. Liam began to unwrap Nora's hand. All she could do was watch.

"It's not your fault, Cam. I shouldn't have been here. My cursed hand is the reason our plan didn't work," Nora said, grinding her teeth together to keep from crying along with Kimi.

"We needed your eyes to make sure Cam didn't have a curse or spell on him," AJ said, "I don't know what we could have done differently."

"I think we really screwed this up," Liam said finishing with the duct tape.

Nora flexed her fingers to make sure they were working. Her right hand was sore but otherwise uninjured.

All of them were silent, trying to think of what to say, but there was nothing left. Staring at the floor, none of them made a move to comfort one another. They simply sat together, as a group, knowing they had failed their friend.

Just then, the silence was broken by a shriek. The noise was coming from down the hall. Rushing to the door, Nora and Liam peeked out to see a dozen spiny creatures marching down the hallway, dragging Fresh along with them. He was kicking and screaming and trying his best to rip out of their grasp, but they held onto him tight.

The leader of the Pukwudgies approached Nora and sensed, '*It seems as though you lost this. We found it outside.*' He had a smug smile on his face.

As the Pukwudgies exchanged something in a language unfamiliar to Nora, they pulled Fresh into the boiler room. She could see now that he had several quills buried in his legs, but he fought the Pukwudgies as if he were uninjured. Their clawed hands dug into his arms and legs along with any other part of him that they got hold of.

'*No! Why?! Let me go!*' Fresh thrashed about like a flopping fish.

The students were beside themselves. They couldn't help but cheer for the ugly little creatures as they shoved Fresh into the small room past the gate.

'*You have learned a valuable lesson about...*' the leader began to sense, but before he could continue, Fresh got his leg free and kicked the Pukwudgie in the knee.

Rubbing his knee, the leader sensed, '*Oh, just throw him in!*'

The Pukwudgies obeyed and tossed Fresh through the wall. He disappeared just as Maria did. They thrust their spears and weapons into the air, hollering. Kimi threw her arms around Cam, who was the closest to her. Liam and Nora bumped fists while AJ wiped his glasses clean, taking in the situation. Ignoring the children, the Pukwudgies spilled out of the room and went back the way they came, chanting something in an unfamiliar language. Watching them leave, Nora could see the smug, triumphant grin on the leader's face.

"I think he really likes bologna," Liam said.

"No one really likes bologna," Nora shot back.

AJ laughed. "I'll leave sandwiches for him every week from now on."

After everyone settled down from the excitement, there was one question left. How were they going to get Maria back from the faerie world.

"Maybe we could link hands and take a look in?" Cam suggested.

"Absolutely not!" a woman hollered from the doorway. Mrs. M practically flew past the children and slammed the gate closed. "Where is the Changeling? What happened?"

CHAPTER 22

Mr. Walker made his way in behind Mrs. M and regarded the students. He pulled out his medical bag and began to treat the wound on Cameron's forehead. The students eyed one another, trying to figure out where to begin.

Eventually, AJ recounted the tale of what had occurred that weekend with the other students interjecting. The frown on Mrs. M's face became more pronounced with each passing minute. Every once in a while she would pace a few steps, her high heels clicking against the cement and her polkadot dress flaring out as she spun around. While the story went on, Mr. Walker patched up Cam's forehead and was inspecting Nora's hand. He left and returned with a small tub of water which he placed some herbs in, before immersing Nora's hand into it, almost up to the elbow. Yeats had grown very small and had curled up into Nora's pocket. Occasionally

Mrs. M would tell the children something they did was reckless, and ask Mr. Walker if he felt the same way. He would always agree.

After they finished the story, everyone, except for Mr. Walker, appeared overwhelmed. Mrs. M had a lot to say and was obviously not used to holding back.

"First, I'd like to reiterate, this was incredibly reckless of all of you. Nora, you never make deals with faeries, from inviting Yeats—yes, I can see you in Nora's pocket—to your house to attempting to trick the Changeling. Once this is all squared away, you will stay far away from faeries and their deals, is that understood?"

Nora nodded, but Yeats popped his head out to argue.

"Yeats will have to be the unfortunate exception. I am not happy with you either, you naughty kitty." She tsked and went on, "Liam, you are not an action star or a medieval knight. Stop jumping into dangerous situations. You would think someone who has a mind to record everything into his notebooks would have more sense than to rush into things. Don't you agree, Mr. Walker?" Mrs. M's fists were in balls but her voice remained level.

"Absolutely," Mr. Walker said, but was obviously very tired, leaning against the wall in his oversized jacket.

Mrs. M continued on her tirade, "Cameron, whatever caused you to talk to the Changeling instead of fleeing from him when you saw him outside, never do that again. He could have done worse than kidnap you and steal some of your hair. AJ, you of all people should know that there are consequences to your actions. I have no idea how you haven't learned more caution by this point. And Kimi, as an upperclassman, you should have been the voice of reason. You should have been a role-model to the other students. What possessed you to go along with any of this?" She did not wait for an answer, it was not one of those kinds of questions.

The students all stared intently at their feet as they were being reprimanded.

"I am very disappointed with all of you for seeking out the Pukwudgies not once but twice after I explicitly told you not to. And then rushing off to the bus yard instead of talking to Mr.Walker or me. You had no idea what dangers could have been waiting for you, you're all lucky to be alive to tell the tale! Once this is over, we will be getting together and doing a great deal more studying and I will be giving all of you exams that must be passed if you ever intend to leave middle school. That's right, we will find a way to keep you here until we are sure you can safely conduct yourselves." Mrs. M finished and took a deep breath.

"And, of course, well done," Mr. Walker said so quietly that it took a moment for the students to process it.

"What?" Liam couldn't believe his ears.

Mr. Walker met Mrs. M's eyes and she sighed.

"Yes, yes, I suppose you were all very clever in your own way and managed to get through this without too much damage, so well done."

There was a wave of relief that washed through the students when they realized they were done being scolded and some of them couldn't help contain their smiles.

"It's not over just yet. Mr. Walker will be driving all of you home while Nora and I prepare for what's next." Mrs. M said matter-of-factly.

Nora nearly jumped at her name. "Me?"

"Yes, dear, I'm afraid we will need your eyes to make sure we have the actual Maria and not the Changeling or some other shapeshifter. We will need one of Maria's belongings to track her down," Mrs. M said.

"Her backpack is on the floor there," Kimi pointed out.

"Excellent. Then off you all go. Yeats, you'll be coming with us, I presume?"

'Me? No, I have a lot of enemies on the other side of that portal,' he sensed.

"Then I suppose you'll entrust Mr. Walker and me to protect Nora?" Mrs. M's eyebrow rose and she crossed her arms over her chest.

Yeats curled around Nora's neck and glared at Mrs. M. He sensed to Nora, *'Salmon sashimi when we get home. Tell the mothers.'*

"If Nora's going, I'm going too!" Liam protested.

"Out of the question," Mrs. M said, "we are only bringing Nora out of necessity. We do not need another student slowing us down."

Liam puffed up, about to say or do something ill-advised, when Mr. Walker stepped in.

"I'm sure you would like to help, but I'm afraid you'd do more harm than good if you came with us, lad. In the faerie realm, Mrs. M and I will have our hands full trying to keep Nora safe while searching for Maria. You'd only slow us down." Mr. Walker's face was solemn but his eyes showed he sympathized with Liam.

"What if this is all my fault? I never should have used that cursed pen in your office!" Liam lamented to Mr. Walker.

Taken back, Mr. Walker put his hand to his chin to try to recall a cursed pen. "The one in my cursed object drawer? All that does is give people diarrhea after they use it."

Liam blanched. "Oh, that explains *that* I guess."

Stepping in, possibly to save Liam some embarrassment, Cam said, "We're not going home until Nora goes home with us."

The other students nodded.

"It's best to get underway anyway," Mrs. M said with a sigh, "I will only consent to you waiting in the East Wing if all of you remain there and do not try to come after us. Anyone who disobeys that will find themselves expelled from school." Mrs. M peered over her glasses at the students.

They all nodded.

"Then it's settled."

Liam bumped knuckles with Nora and wished her luck. Then Kimi hugged Nora while AJ and Cam waved awkward goodbyes. As soon as the students left, Mr. Walker took a vial full of fluorescent green liquid out of his bag. He removed the stopper and tilted it, pouring the contents onto Maria's backpack.

While Mr. Walker coated the bag, Mrs. M spoke. "Now, Nora, be very careful when we get into the faerie realm. Nothing is as it seems. Even if your eyes will be of use to you, they may also show you things you do not wish to see. Sometimes up is down and down is up. Stay close to me and Mr. Walker. Do not eat or drink anything on the other side and do not talk to anyone or anything. Do you understand?" Mrs. M seemed very stern, but then she put her hand on Nora's shoulder and sensed. *'I know all of this is frightening, but Yeats will be with you and he would do anything to have a pampered house cat lifestyle.'*

'House cat? How dare you! I am a mighty Cat Sith. Feared by all who...'

Nora rubbed his cheek and he began to purr. He soon forgot about his protests.

Mr. Walker let out a laugh and Mrs. M could not help but smile. Lifting the now glowing bag, Mr. Walker held it out to show a green, luminescent line stopping at the wall. Nodding, Mrs. M stepped through the wall followed by Mr. Walker. Nora's heart was racing. She knew she had to follow to help out, but after all of the warnings, she was worried about what she would find on the other side. Focusing on Yeats' warm purrs around her neck, she took a deep breath and stepped through the wall.

There was an immediate dizzying sensation that almost caused Nora to lose her lunch. She was suddenly standing in a forest with trees taller than she had ever seen. They reminded her of pictures of redwood forests in California, but she had never seen them in person. The air was suddenly much cooler than the boiler room which was a little warmer than comfortable. The whir of the furnace in the background was replaced by the buzzing of insects and an occasional bird-like noise. A slight mist hung in the air around them and everything smelled of ozone like after it rains.

When she shifted her attention up to see the tops of the trees, she suddenly saw that the sky seemed to be reflecting the trees like a pond would the sky. It was very alarming to see the opposite and gave her instant vertigo. She almost fell to her side, but Mrs. M caught her arm.

"It takes some getting used to," Mrs. M said, "Let's try to get out of here as quickly as possible."

Nora nodded, but she felt too woozy to respond. They followed the light shining from Maria's backpack into the woods. Out of the corner of her eye, Nora would occasionally see what she thought was a face peeking out from behind a tree, but when she tried to focus on it, it would vanish. Whatever was spying on them was even better at camouflaging than the

Pukwudgies. Underneath her shoes, Nora could feel the soft moss which covered the ground instead of grass.

All varieties of mushroom popped up from the ground but were only visible when they were almost stepping on them. The mist was getting thicker the further they went, which the fireflies lit up brighter than day, making it appear to be a solid mass they were walking through. When one of the fireflies got close, Nora realized it wasn't a firefly at all, but a glowing, miniscule faerie. It was just like a miniature person, wearing leaves for clothing, and an acorn hat. Its little wings lit up with a yellow light when it flapped them and emitted a buzzing noise.

She hadn't been sure what to expect every time they talked about the faerie world, but there was no way she could have imagined this. Every inch of the faerie realm was exciting and new. Watching the twinkling faeries, she wanted to go after them and explore the dense woods.

"Stay close!" Mrs. M barked before Nora even realized she was falling behind.

Rubbing her eyes, she suddenly saw a murky bog beside the path, the way she had previously wanted to go. Now she couldn't understand why she had ever wanted to slog through it.

'Will-o-wisps .' Yeats sensed to her, *'They get people lost and trapped in muck so they can slowly devour them.'*

Nora swallowed. *'Those cute little pixies?'*

Yeats swatted at one that came by. *'Cute? I thought you had faerie eyes.'*

Squinting her eyes at one when it went by, she suddenly saw that it had greyish skin and a nasty, mischievous expression on its face. It also had dozens of needle-like teeth that it readily showed off when it flew past. Shuddering, Nora rushed to catch up with the teachers.

Mr. Walker had stopped to put the backpack down. They had reached a wall of vines, but the light was telling them to continue. Mrs. M frowned. She then pulled a thin dagger out of a pocket in her skirt and sliced at the vines in a quick motion. They fell apart as if they were made of paper. Before them there were two tunnels, and the light of Maria's backpack was bringing them down the one to the left.

"Give me the backpack," Mrs. M said to Mr. Walker, "I will get Maria and bring her here."

Mr. Walker nodded and handed over the backpack. He then made himself comfortable on a nearby rock and patted the one next to him for Nora to join him. Even though she wasn't sure why Mrs. M would insist on going into the cave by herself, Nora was not in any position to argue and Mrs. M had left their sight before she could ask any questions.

"Is she going to be OK by herself?" Nora asked.

"I always find it's best to trust Mrs. M's instincts," Mr. Walker smiled. He then pulled out a box of yogurt-covered raisins and offered some to Nora.

"I thought we weren't supposed to eat or drink anything here," Nora said.

"Oh, that's faerie food. If you eat or drink faerie food you will be stuck here forever." Mr. Walker examined the box of raisins and shook them. "You don't think that applies to food we bring in too, does it?"

Nora shrugged. Mr. Walker closed the box and returned it to his bag.

"I guess it's better safe than sorry," He said.

Yeats curled up on Nora's lap and she petted him absentmindedly while they waited. Mr. Walker tried to play some sort of number game with Nora to make the time pass quicker, but it was hard for her to focus on anything.

The lights twirling in the mists were so mesmerizing. Each time she was about to drift off, Mr. Walker would nudge her and tell her it was her turn. She was starting to get annoyed by his constant badgering. There was also something hiding behind one of the trees that she just could not get a good look at, no matter how hard she tried. If she could only focus her eyes a little bit more...but her eyelids were so heavy.

CHAPTER 23

She must have dozed off for a second, since she woke to Mr. Walker tapping her on the shoulder. He was standing and fidgeting as if he were worried about something while trying to help her to her feet.

"Someone is coming out of the cave. Be prepared to do exactly as I say," Mr. Walker said quietly to Nora.

Nodding, she got to her feet while Yeats readjusted to sit on her shoulder. She squinted into the darkness which made up both sides of the cave. Nora thought of the cave entrances as large nostrils on a giant sleeping head. Rubbing her eyes, she tried to shake the murky feeling clogging her mind.

Just as Mr. Walker had predicted, a person stepped out from the darkness. She had long hair, tan skin and dark eyes.

"Mrs. M told me to go on ahead," Maria said.

Mr. Walker breathed a sigh of relief. "Very good to see you, young lady."

"She said we could go on without her and she'd catch up." Maria said.

At first Nora was glad to see Maria's familiar face, but then she realized there was something off about it. Her eyes were a little too big, and a little too dark. The way she enunciated her words was too specific and there was a slight smile in the corner of her mouth that Nora had never seen before. Nora had, in fact, never seen Maria genuinely smile before—there was always a sadness behind it. The more she studied Maria's face the more she knew it was not Maria.

"All right then," Mr. Walker said, gathering up his bag and zipping up his oversized jacket to be underway.

"What did you do to Mrs. M?" Nora asked all of a sudden.

"I don't know what you mean, like I told you..." Maria's mouth began to expand wider than it should and revealed a few too many teeth. She moved her hand in a swiping motion at Nora, but nothing happened. She then looked perplexed.

"If you were hoping for the curse on Nora's hand to help you, I removed it," Mr. Walker said.

Nora glanced at her hand. She did not realize it was completely cured, but the red finger marks were gone, and she was glad for it.

Becoming enraged, Maria let out a fierce scream and her limbs began to grow longer and sharper than they were previously. She was transforming into a dreadful beast with long insectoid legs and claws, and it was not a pretty sight. Her face elongated to make a pointy beak like a bird with rows of teeth underneath. As its legs grew, they made popping sounds and stretched outward causing its body to rise up. While morphing and growing, the Changeling let out wretched screeches to make all aware the process was painful. Before the Changeling was finished with its transformation, however, Yeats took his chance to attack.

In seconds, Yeats grew to a massive size, larger than a semi-truck and scooped the changeling up with his paw like a mouse. He then bit down on it and there was a disturbing crunch. He spat the Changeling back onto the ground where it lay in a twitching heap of malformed limbs.

Nora and Mr. Walker were too shocked and horrified to move. Mr. Walker had stepped in front of Nora protectively where he remained stunned.

'*He'll be fine,*' Yeats sensed while returning back to the size of a house cat. 'It'll take a while for him to heal that, though.'

Just then, vines began to rise up from the ground and wrap themselves around the Changeling's deformed body. The vines tightened and dragged the creature down into the earth. As the ground rumbled, each of them stepped away to avoid being swallowed up in the dirt rolling over it. In a matter of minutes, the entire creature was gone and there was only a darkened bit of dirt left to show that anything was out of place.

'*Guards reclaiming their prisoner,*' Yeats sensed.

"Well, that was...something," Mr. Walker said after a pause. "Everyone all right?"

Before Nora could respond, she felt herself being pulled by the back of her shirt. It all happened so fast that she almost felt like she was flying through the air in a dream where if she could just twitch the right muscle at the right time, she would be able to control it. The trees flew by in a blur of browns that she desperately hoped she would not crash into. Somehow, everything came to a halt all at once. She was sitting on the moss ground next to a red-spotted mushroom which was at least two feet tall. It was by far the largest one she had ever seen, and there was a woman standing before her.

She was the most beautiful woman Nora had ever seen. Her skin was pale and smooth as glass. Pointed ears stuck out from long flowing hair that reminded her of Maria's, but thinner and more like a gossamer cloak. Her eyes had a reddish glimmer as she stared at Nora's shoulder. Her blue silken gown glowed like moonlight around her, lighting up her pale skin and purple lips. It was hard for Nora to take her eyes off of the woman, but there was something unnerving about her, like she wasn't actually there.

'Yeats, you have finally returned,' the woman said in a silvery voice. She moved as if she were under water, her arms gliding back and forth to keep herself afloat and her silk sleeves flowing along with her. It took a second for Nora to realize the woman was addressing Yeats.

'Only momentarily,' Yeats sensed from atop Nora's shoulder.

'And you have brought a snack? I am famished,' the Blue Lady slid forward and ran her tongue across her jagged canines.

'This child? No, no, it's an interesting story actually. It all starts with...Run!' Yeats sensed to Nora with an urgency that caused her to remember her legs while he threw himself at the woman in a flurry of teeth and claws.

Not entirely sure where she had come from, Nora picked a direction and ran. Anything was better than waiting to be eaten by the scary faerie lady. So, she rushed ahead as fast as her feet could carry her. The ground was soft beneath her feet. Once she almost slid into a marsh on the side of the mossy path, but she managed to regain her balance and slip through the thick tree trunks. By the time she tripped over a tree root, she had lost sight of the

Blue Lady and Yeats even though there was less fog in this area. Luckily, moss is good for breaking people's falls.

Sitting for a moment, she caught her breath and looked up at the strange sky. There weren't stars but moving, glowing orbs, larger than the will-o-wisps Yeats had pointed out. If everything wasn't so unusual, it would have been nice to sit and simply watch. Unfortunately, Nora realized she was alone in a world she knew nothing about. She felt small and stupid and wished Liam were there to encourage her. Trying to think of what he would do in the situation, she pictured him sitting beside her and making a joke that this was probably their worst field trip. Even worse than the Tupperware museum they visited in third grade.

'Land of Faeries, wouldn't say the weather was good or bad, but could do without everything trying to eat me. One out of Five stars, would not go back,' Nora pictured Liam saying and couldn't help but laugh.

Feeling encouraged by Liam's imagined joke, she got to her feet and began walking in the direction she thought she had come from. Even though she was lost in a forest in a world entirely different from her own, something about the idea of getting back to Liam to tell him all about what had happened kept her going. She hoped Yeats would be all right after tangling with the Blue Lady, but knew she had to focus on continuing in one direction to make any progress. After what felt like an eternity of stepping over thick roots and avoiding low branches, Nora's feet were beginning to hurt and she was getting tired.

She thought about sitting again, but didn't want to fall asleep, alone in the faerie woods. Her eyes were growing blurry, but all of a sudden she saw a glowing line in the distance, similar to the one Mr. Walker had used to find Maria. Shrugging, she decided to follow it and hoped to find her friends on the other end. It did not take long before she saw three figures emerge from the fog. All of a sudden, one of the three ran up to her and wrapped her arms around her. It was Maria. Nora almost cried tears of joy. The foggy sensation in her head started to clear.

Triumphantly, Maria held up a small vase with flowers affixed to it. It had been delicately painted with reds and pinks to make the details pop out. It was also glowing green. She immediately recognized their combined art project.

"I brought it home to paint it. I forgot to show you. It was in my backpack!" Maria exclaimed.

"What a relief," Mr. Walker patted his balding head with a handkerchief. "Quickly now, let's go home."

"What about Yeats?" Nora asked, looking back through the woods.

Mrs. M lifted her glasses and examined the thickening fog rolling in. "I'm afraid he'll have to find his way back on his own."

Nora didn't want to accept it, but she knew Mrs. M was right. They didn't have any way to find him, and they couldn't go wandering through the dangerous forest in hopes of running into him. They returned to the area they had entered where a circle of mushrooms marked the way to the boiler room. The air twisted and swirled between the mushrooms just like it did on the wall of the boiler room. Mrs. M and Mr. Walker insisted on Maria and Nora going first.

As soon as they stepped through, they were greeted by a cheer from the other students. AJ, Kimi, Cam, and Liam rushed in for a group hug with Maria and Nora. Nora was taken back at first, but then was so relieved to see her friends that she practically jumped for joy.

"Ouch, AJ," Cam exclaimed, pulling away as he got shocked.

AJ shrugged and the other students laughed.

Once the teachers stepped through, Mrs. M reprimanded the students for not remaining in the Secret Wing like they were told to. When Mrs. M went to close the iron gate, Nora protested.

"How will Yeats get back?"

"Yeats is still in there?" Liam asked, causing Nora to realize he cared for the cat more than he let on. "What happened? We have to get him back."

"I'm sorry, but we cannot simply leave the gate open. We can check daily. Yeats will find his way back eventually," Mrs. M said assuredly.

Nora didn't like Mrs. M's curt response, but she knew there was no arguing with her at this point. They had managed to get rid of a dangerous changeling, survived a mysterious world full of monsters, and got their friend back. It had been an eventful day and by the rumbling of her stomach, Nora knew it was past dinner time.

"Mr. Walker will be driving Nora, Liam, and AJ home. I'll be taking Kimiko, Maria, and Cameron. Get your things, we are leaving immediately. We will have a full discussion about this in the morning. I'm afraid you will all have to miss some of your regular classes so we can debrief you on this situation," Mrs. M did not wait for a reply or make sure the students were following her out of the boiler room.

AJ sat in the front seat of Mr. Walker's car where he was permitted to flip through the radio stations. Either none of the stations were playing anything to his liking or he was intent on flipping. Mr. Walker didn't seem to be bothered by it. Nora didn't have much time to talk to Liam on the way home, but she promised to give him all the details in the morning. For now, she was trying to think up another excuse to her family on how

Yeats got out again, but she couldn't think of anything aside from her being careless.

CHAPTER 24

The next day, the Wyrd students went through every minute detail of the previous day's adventures. Mrs. M and Mr. Walker quizzed them as if they should have studied for a test. They were able to help one another with some details, but others were fuzzy. None knew why the Pukwudgies changed their minds and came to the aid of the students. Nor did they understand why Fresh was so eager to make an agreement in the first place. But, somehow things had worked out.

Mrs. M explained to Nora and Maria that the longer they were away from the faerie realm, the more blurry their memories would be of what had happened there. So Nora made sure to give a detailed account of everything with Liam recording it. For some reason she felt a chill go down her spine whenever she thought of the Blue Lady and what would have befallen her if Yeats wasn't there to help. The unnatural monster Fresh had morphed into paled in comparison to the eerie, blue woman's swimming motions. She hoped she would forget about it like Mrs. M said or the blue woman would surely haunt her nightmares.

After the debriefing and relaxation time in the calming room by Mr. Walker's office, Mrs. M gave each of the students a schedule with detailed lessons on safety techniques, magical creatures, and unearthly realms. She would be giving them weekly tests to make sure they were understanding the material. Mr. Walker often glanced at them sympathetically, but Mrs. M was determined to make sure no students put themselves in harm's way again.

By the end of the week, they were given clearance to reunite the slime creatures in the bus yard (with teacher supervision, of course). The teachers spoke with their parents about a community service project that had to do with cleaning the marshlands, so before long they found themselves back at the school bus yard.

The day was unnaturally warm for the season, with clouds threatening to rain all morning. The air grew heavy the closer they got to the bus yard and they knew it had to do with the emotional effect of the slime monster. There was less anger now and more of an overwhelming sadness, like a deep, never ending hole had opened up and there was no way to fill it back in. As they approached the marshes, Nora felt like she had lost something very important to her but couldn't place what it was.

AJ, Cam, Nora, and Maria huddled around Kimi who was holding a plastic fish bowl with a ball of black goop in it. Frightened by all of the movement, Inky had remained curled up since they removed him from the larger tank. Liam stood to the side, ready to sketch whatever he saw, and the teachers remained back a ways to allow the students some independence.

Kimi leaned down to the edge of the pavement where the marsh began to encroach. She popped open the lid of the fish tank and tilted it towards the marsh. '*Goodbye Inky,*' Kimi sensed, '*it was nice to meet you, I hope you have plenty of...whatever you eat out here.*' Inky remained in a ball, refusing to unstick itself from the side of the tank. '*Come on little guy, you can go home now.*' Sniffling, Kimi was clearly holding back tears, but it was unclear if she felt strongly for inky or if the sadness from the slime creature was making her emotional.

A sudden popping noise and then a splash startled them and nearly caused Kimi to drop the bowl. After steadying her hands, Inky's eyes poked out of his ball and he slid to the very edge of the bowl. The larger slime creature oozed up and popped its head out of the murky water. With a jolt, it suddenly lurched forward. Nora wanted to leap back, but knew they were there to support Kimi in releasing Inky, so she held firm with the others. In an instant, the gooey creature was less than a foot away from them. Stopping just at the edge of the water, its eyes protruded from its slimy body like two wiffle balls on pikes. The white eyes began to swirl with colors as it examined Inky.

Slipping down the edge of the tank, inky plopped into the water beside the larger slime. Goopy limbs scooped it up and held it in front of the swirling eyes which had become a rainbow kaleidoscope of colors. Both slimes changed from a deep purple, so dark that it appeared to be black, to luminescent almost translucent globs. The heaviness in the air evaporated in an instant and they were all left with feelings of immense joy.

The slimes swiveled their eyes to look at the children one last time before slipping back into the shallow water, vanishing beneath the surface. Nora returned Liam's grin. He had put his pencil down to watch the reunion.

He had been right. It was just like the mother and baby raccoon who were desperate to be reunited. It was an amazing feeling that Nora knew she would hold onto for the rest of her life.

As the days and weeks passed by, the students grew closer together through their shared experiences. The comic book store became their weekly hangout spot for board games, which AJ was happy to teach them. Each of them made excuses to spend time with one another in school as well. Nora enjoyed art class with Maria, PE with Cam, and mentor time with Kimi. Of course, they all had extra classes in the Secret Wing since Mrs. M wanted to make sure they kept up with their supernatural studies. Even though she was strict with them, it was obvious she was proud of their achievements, and she once mentioned that they showed more promise than any Wyrd students she'd had.

It wasn't long before Liam returned to the school bus. Although Skip was never friendly, he got rid of the arranged seating and no longer yelled at the students for small infractions. The whole school calmed down considerably after the unexplained disappearance of the purple slime from students' backpacks or lockers and even teachers' desks. Mrs. M and Mr. Walker never disclosed to the Wyrd students how they managed that caper, but grinned devilishly whenever asked. Since the fights ended, the school administrators and parents chalked the whole incident up to 'back to school blues' made worse by the delayed opening that year.

About a month after everything had settled down, the desk drawer in Mr. Walker's office containing cursed objects was sporting a shiny new lock. Somehow a specific pen had gone missing and there was a short-lived stomach bug making its way through a few students who had coincidently been disrespectful to Nora (Ava, Penelope, and Tracy to name a few).

Although all of the Wyrd students denied any knowledge of the missing cursed pen, Nora suspected it was Maria's way of thanking her for everything.

Liam had gone through 3 new notebooks of their adventures in the first few weeks of school. There was a lot to record and draw. He followed Nora's suggestion of categorizing each year at their middle school by color and designating a shelf for them. Their first year was red for no other reason than the fact that Liam had started with a red notebook. Although there were minor Wyrd occurrences during the rest of the school year, nothing compared to their adventures fighting the Changeling. Every once in a while Nora saw a Pukwudgie out of the corner of her eye at recess. Whenever she did, she'd make sure to drop crackers or candy for them. And, after Halloween that year, the students got together to dump their bags at the end of the walkways as a special thanks.

Mr. Walker did his best to keep the library organized with Yeats gone, but he couldn't even keep his own office clean. Nora began to avoid the library, which had become drab and lonely to her. Mrs. M made it clear to Nora that no students were ever allowed to wander through the faerie gate again and that Yeats' own magic would get in the way of the tracking spell they had used to find Maria. Even though the teachers tried their best to reassure Nora that Yeats was in his natural environment and would return when he was ready, Nora could not help but grow more and more worried. Each day she checked the boiler room, but there was no sign of a cat.

Her family was sad along with her at the disappearance of their pet. They put up flyers and walked the neighborhood, even though Nora knew it would do no good. Her moms tried to make her feel better by saying that maybe he was picked up by his original owners, but that didn't even cheer up Emaline.

Days became shorter and nights longer. Although Nora was keeping busy with school, Wyrd studies, and her new friends, she still felt as though something was missing. After finishing her homework, and getting ready for bed, Nora threw her heavy quilt over her head. She had forgotten to shut the lights off, but didn't want to get back up now that she was nestled beneath the heavy bedspread. Closing her eyes, her mind drifted to warmer days with a cat curled up next to her, purring. She pictured Yeats' sleek fur and green crescent eyes blinking sleepily at her from the other side of the bed. She could almost feel him there, his soft body pressed up against hers. Lifting the blanket, she peered out to see a black bundle beside her. She rubbed her eyes. Opened them again. He was still there.

Yeats opened his mouth wide in a yawn. '*Salmon sashimi,*' he sensed.

"Yeats!" Nora squeaked.

'*I was promised salmon sashimi,*' Yeats repeated, rolling his head back lazily and exposing his stomach for rubs.

Petting his belly exuberantly, Nora sensed, '*But how did you get here?*'

Yeats blinked. He crept up to Nora's face until he was only inches away and sensed, '*But, Noh-Rah, I was invited. Don't you remember?*'